T0354324

The Ghosts

of Cotton Row

Louis J. Cuccia

iUniverse, Inc.
New York   Bloomington

The Ghosts of Cotton Row

Original Edit by Arlene Uslander
www.Uslander.net

iUniverse books may be ordered through booksellers or by contacting:

iUniverse
1663 Liberty Drive
Bloomington, IN 47403
www.iuniverse.com
1-800-Authors (1-800-288-4677)

ISBN: 978-1-4502-3558-7 (pbk)
ISBN: 978-1-4502-3557-0 (cloth)
ISBN: 978-1-4502-3559-4 (ebk)

Library of Congress Control Number: 2010908282

Printed in the United States of America

iUniverse rev. date: 7/7/2010

PREFACE

The city of Memphis, Tennessee, was founded in 1819. Sitting on the banks of the Mississippi River, the city grew into a major transportation port. In the early 1950s, 40 percent of all the cotton sold and traded in the nation came through Memphis. The city was the largest cotton market on the Mississippi River and considered the cotton capital of the South. Cotton was king.

As synthetic fibers became more available in the late fifties, the cotton market began to decline. The racial tensions of the sixties followed, and Memphis went into a downward economic spiral. The city began to lose its identity. The traditional Cotton Carnival, a festival and riverside fair similar to the Mardi Gras in New Orleans, slowly faded away as the city changed and cotton became far less important. Once the barges stopped coming in, the merchants on Cotton Row found it necessary to close their shops and either leave Memphis or start a new career.

It was in 1954 when a young man known to most as just Elvis hit the music scene. He was born in Tupelo, Mississippi, and his family had moved to Memphis in 1948. He shocked audiences with his hip gyrations and rockabilly music, a blend of country and rhythm and blues. He recorded his first record at Sun Studio on Union Avenue in Memphis. The studio is now a National Historic Landmark, and it's considered the birthplace of rock 'n' roll. It took city officials and politicians another decade to push for a downtown reconstruction centered on that little strip where W. C. Handy had performed a new type of music in 1909. That strip was Beale Street, and the music was the blues.

Some of the buildings along Cotton Row are still standing. Some have been torn down to make way for parking lots and new businesses. Some have been converted into restaurants and tourist shops. The cotton merchants and porters who once walked the streets of Cotton Row have long been gone. Their significance in the early growth and economic shaping of Memphis should never be forgotten. It is often said that they still walk the streets at night and that they talk among themselves about when cotton was king. They will forever be known as the ghosts of Cotton Row. This book is fiction. People, dates, and places mentioned in this book are not meant to be historically accurate.

CHAPTER 1

The Gumshoe Detective

OFFICERS JACK MILLS AND Dave Drake cut through the South Second Street alley between Monroe and Union avenues. Even at 3:00 AM, the humid air glued the shirts of their dark blue police uniforms to their bodies. If the weather stations were right, 2007 would be one of the hottest summers on record. The annual Memphis in May Festival had just ended and ushered in the climbing temperatures of June. The monthlong festival is one of the city's largest moneymakers and is known nationwide for its World Championship Barbecue Cooking Contest. This year two hundred fifty teams of barbecue venders from twenty states and several countries filled the thirty-three acres of Tom Lee Park, and an estimated ninety thousand people attended the competition. Jack, for one, was glad it was over.

Jack stepped out for what seemed like the hundredth time to check the iron gate, the chain, and the padlock. He wiped the sweat from his face with a handkerchief and blotted his short-cropped dark hair. The odor of smoking ribs still lingered in the heavy, moist air as he shook the gate of the landmark Rendezvous restaurant. He took a deep breath and could almost taste the tender pork. His mouth began to water. Jack had eaten many times at the restaurant and had become friends with its owner, Charles Vergos. He had listened more than once to Charles telling the story about how the Rendezvous opened in the South Second Street alley in 1948 and how its famous recipe for highly seasoned dry-rub ribs had developed. Charles always ended the story with how Elvis often had those ribs flown in while performing in Las Vegas.

A few blocks south of the Rendezvous was the Beale Street Historic District, known as the Home of the Blues. It was a night haven for visitors who wanted to listen to some of the best blues in the south. B.B. King's Blues Club, Blues City Café, and the Rum Boogie Café were all known for their music, food, and beer. The Beale Street District was part of Jack and Dave's weekend gumshoe patrol.

It was during the last week of the Memphis in May Festival that Jack had discovered the body.

He and Dave had been driving down Riverside Drive along the front of Tom Lee Park. From the car, Jack had seen a silhouette of someone seated on a park bench facing the river. At 4:00 AM, a lone person in the park required a stop-and-see. When they investigated, they had found an unshaven male with a single bullet hole in his forehead. From the looks of his tattered clothes and bag, he appeared to be one of the homeless that often walked around the edges of the festival trying to sample the free food and drinks. Later, ballistics indicated that the murder weapon was a .38-caliber handgun. The gun had been fired at close range. No other information surfaced during the preliminary investigation.

The *Commercial Appeal*, the local newspaper, didn't run the story on the front page. Such a murder wasn't major news. The short article that did appear simply stated that a homeless white male approximately sixty years old was found shot to death on Riverside Drive. No suspects. Investigation pending. There had been a similar shooting earlier the same week on Union Avenue. The first homicide had taken place near the Memphis Publishing Company that had housed the original Ford Motor Company assembly plant back in 1959. The first victim was a fifty-year-old homeless black male, known as John "Skipper" Doe, due to the sailing hat that always covered his white-haired head. Same MO. One shot with a .38-caliber handgun to the forehead. No suspects.

Jack and Dave had spoken to Skipper many times on the street. Jack considered him an eccentric, but pleasant man. Skipper had become something of an icon on Union Avenue. Lots of people had known him. The business owners around Union Avenue had told Jack that Skipper would look after the parked cars on Union Avenue, and that he often washed windshields for a couple of bucks. Jack had often bought him a cup of coffee and asked about what was going on in the area. He knew that Skipper was street-smart and would know if anything was going down. He would never tell Jack straight out what he knew, but he would clue Jack in by saying something like, "I'd stay away from the Firestone and Manassas area." That, of course, was exactly where the police needed to be.

Jack had thought that Skipper's demise was part of a broken car or drug deal. Now, he wasn't so sure. He had last seen Skipper the night before his homicide in front of the National Historic Landmark Sun Studio, where Elvis had recorded "That's All Right" on the Sun label in 1954. Skipper's conversation that night had been more erratic than usual and was difficult to follow. Something was obviously wrong on the Union Avenue strip, but little information was gained from their conversation.

The two murders lingered in Jack's thoughts as he peered down the alley toward the Peabody Hotel. The street was quiet. He sighed, tried to clear his mind of the gloom he felt, and returned to the patrol car. Dave sat and sipped his Dunkin' Donuts black coffee. There was little conversation between them after 3:00 AM. Jack pulled the patrol car through the alley and stopped at Union Avenue next to the Holiday Inn. To his right, he saw a shadow dash into a dark alcove of the Peabody Hotel.

"Did you see something over there?" asked Jack, motioning across the street toward the hotel.

"No, nothing," Dave said.

"I know I saw something. Better check it out."

Dave looked at his watch: 3:24 AM.

Switching the car's lights on, Jack turned right and eased along the street. "There! Someone is pressed against the Lansky Brothers entrance."

3

Approaching carefully, Jack pulled the car up to the left curb and shined his flashlight into the face of a white male.

"Police. Step out where we can see you," ordered Jack.

Shading his eyes from the light, the man slowly stepped out.

"Keep your hands where we can see them. What are you doing here?" Jack asked.

"Nothing," the man said.

Jack made a quick assessment. Middle-aged white male, around five-feet ten inches tall, approximately one hundred-forty pounds, with long dark hair. He was dressed in a pair of faded blue jeans, a checkered blue shirt, and dirty tennis shoes. His shirttails hung down over his waistline, causing Jack concern about whether the guy was carrying a concealed weapon.

"Place your right hand on your head, and lift your shirt up with your left hand. Now, turn around slowly," Jack demanded.

The man pulled his shirt up, exposing his bare skin, and turned around as directed.

"You have any weapons?" questioned Jack, who made a mental note that the man had no bulging pockets.

"No."

"You can drop your shirt, but keep your hands out of your pockets," Jack said.

Seeing that the man posed no threat, Jack stepped out of the car. He was a big man, and his six-foot two-inch, one hundred-ninety-pound muscular frame made the guy in front of him look small. Dave got out of the car as well and stood beside the passenger door so he could get a full view of the street.

"For your safety and mine, I'm going to give you a quick pat down. Turn around, place your hands on the side of the building, and spread your legs."

The man obeyed.

Feeling nothing in the man's pockets, Jack continued his questioning.

"You can turn around now. What are you doing here?" Jack asked again.

"Walking."

"From where?"

"Union Mission."

"You staying at the mission?"

"Yep."

"You have any identification on you?"

"No."

"Got a name?"

"Ted."

"Ted what?"

"Meyer."

Jack turned to Dave. "Give dispatch a call and have them contact the Union Avenue Mission. See if they have any information on a Ted Meyer staying there."

Dave nodded and stepped back into the patrol car.

"Where you from, Ted?"

"St. Louis."

"Where you going?"

"Jackson."

"Jackson, Tennessee, or Jackson, Mississippi?"

"Mississippi." Ted kept his head down, not wanting to make eye contact.

"You have some family in Jackson?"

"Yes, family and friends."

"Why were you hiding?"

"Don't want to be picked up. Going to Jackson," Ted said.

"See anybody on the street while you were walking around?"

"Just you guys."

Dave returned to his earlier spot on the passenger side of the patrol car. "Checks out. Man named Pete Johnson said Ted is staying at the mission. Not there now. Didn't sign out. Must have slipped past him. The door can be opened from the inside, but you have to buzz to get back in."

"He was sleeping," Ted remarked.

"Ted, I want you to listen to me. It's dangerous on these streets at night. There have been two homicides in this area. Get in the car, and we'll drive you back to the mission."

"I'd rather walk."

Jack knew that was coming. No one wanted to ride in a police car. Most figured they would be taken to jail.

"Ted, don't make this hard. Get inside the car, and we'll drive you over to the mission."

Ted's eyes looked up for the first time. Jack could see the fear on his face.

"Do you know where we are?" Jack asked.

"No, I got turned around."

"You're on Union Avenue. The mission is three blocks down on your right. We just want to be sure you make it back to the mission okay."

Ted nodded in agreement.

Once Ted was in the backseat, Jack entered the patrol car and closed the soundproof glass window between the back and front seats.

"What'd you think?" Dave asked.

"Sounds on the up-and-up. Classic traveler. In and out of town. A strange place. Can't sleep. Probably a little paranoid and thinks somebody's out to get him. This time, he may be right," answered Jack.

The three-block drive was at a snail's pace. Pulling up to the Union Avenue Mission's front door, Jack got out of the patrol car and helped Ted from the backseat. He buzzed for the guard. A round face peered through the glass door.

"Officer Jack Mills," Jack announced. "Police dispatch spoke with a Pete Johnson."

"That's me."

The door opened, and both men stepped inside.

"Ted, you can't leave here at night without signing out," commented the guard. "He must have slipped out when I went to the bathroom," he remarked to Jack. "Hard to keep track of these guys, you know? Don't understand why they always want to run around at night when the world is sleeping. Don't make sense, does it?"

"He was sleeping," Ted quietly stated.

"I was not! I was in the bathroom," Pete said.

"Ted, I want you to go on back to your bunk. And don't let this happen again," the guard said.

Ted walked down the hall, past a long table, and through a metal detector. The light remained green.

Jack made a quick visual assessment of Pete Johnson. Five-foot-six, elderly black man. Heavy. Maybe two hundred-sixty pounds. He was bald on top, with short white hair on the sides and back of his head. A small scar ran below his left ear. Blue pants and blue shirt. A South Memphis Security Service emblem was stitched over his shirt pocket and on his left sleeve.

"How long have you been here, Mr. Johnson?"

"About a month. I retired last year. Started this job to help out at home. I've been assigned here until they can find a replacement for Jim. My wife's been sick, and we need the money for expenses. You're not going to report this, are you? I need this job. I'll be more careful next time," Pete said.

"No harm done, Mr. Johnson. But you may want to put your chair in front of the door," Jack said with a grin.

The guard stared at Jack for a moment before he got the message, and he smiled back at Jack. "Yes, sir," he said. "Good idea. I'll do that."

"Tell me something, Mr. Johnson. Have you seen anybody hanging around who doesn't stay here?" asked Jack.

"There was that detective who came around after the murder at the river. You know, when that man got shot in the head?"

"Yeah, I know. Had the man who was murdered been staying here?" questioned Jack.

"No. But this guy I'm talking about brought the victim's picture by and asked if I knew him."

"Did this fellow with the picture tell you who he was?" asked Jack.

"I believe he said his name was Lou. Yeah, that's it. Lou," replied Pete.

Jack had heard that with all the pressure from city hall, Lou Cros might be assigned to the homicides. "Does the name Lou Cros ring a bell with you?" Jack asked.

"Yeah, that's it. I remember now. He said, Cros with one *S*. Nice man. Offered me a piece of gum."

"Anyone else come to mind?"

"No, just him. That was it. Most of these people are only here for a day or two. Take a shower, get a meal and bed, and move on."

"You mentioned that you'll be here until they find a replacement for Jim. Are you speaking of Jim Damos?" Jack asked.

"Oh, Jim Dandy? Jim Dandy, that's what I call him. He lives out in Whitehaven. He helped me get this job. He turned seventy-two last January. He finally decided to retire. You know Jim Dandy?"

"Yes, Mr. Damos was here a long time," Jack replied.

"Funny, that detective asked about him too."

"I would hope so," Jack said with a smile.

Pete stared at Jack again, and then he laughed. "Oh yeah, I see."

"Well, Mr. Johnson, my partner and I will be stopping by from time to time. You have our number if you need it?"

"Yes, sir. It is right by the phone. Thanks for bringing Ted back, and thanks for the other thing we talked about. My wife and I appreciate it."

Jack really regretted that he hadn't been by the mission more often, but he knew there was a fine line between how often you could stop by the mission without scaring away the people who really needed the services it could provide. It was better to have them in a shelter than on the street. Especially now. Since the two homicides. Stepping back into the patrol car, he found Dave listening to the police radio.

"Something there for us?" asked Jack.

"No, it's a problem over by the projects on Brown Street. Domestic violence. Sounds like they have it under control," Dave said.

"Guard inside said Lou Cros had been by asking questions about the

Riverside victim. I'm a little surprised Captain Smitters would put him in charge of an investigation so early after his return."

"Yeah, me too. Have you heard how he's doing?"

"No, not really. I guess the captain feels he's okay. I heard one story that he had a breakdown and another one that he just took extended leave. I really don't know what to think."

By seven in the morning, the two cops had covered their beat several times without incident. As soon as they heard from their replacements, they headed in. Jack was about to open his car door at the precinct when the dispatcher's voice squawked through the police radio.

"Captain wants to see you two, ASAP," the dispatcher said.

"Ten-four. We're on our way," Jack replied.

Dave gave Jack a quick look. "What'd we do now?"

Entering the precinct, Jack and Dave headed straight to Captain John Smitters's office. Jack gave a knuckle knock on the open door, and he and Dave received a come-on-in motion followed by another one to sit. They took a seat and waited for Smitters to finish what he was doing. They both knew that the captain was a retired Navy SEAL, and that the man was all business. Jack couldn't help but stare at his short-cropped blond hair. Every hair was perfect. He was always amazed at how much Smitters resembled Arnold Schwarzenegger. He was similar in height, and he had the same broad shoulders, square jaw, and muscular build.

Lou Cros was seated in a chair against the far wall. Lou sported his regular uniform. Light brown coat, tan pants, white shirt, open collar, striped blue tie pulled down about three inches below his neck. Lou was about the same age as Captain Smitters, around sixty, but much shorter, around five-foot-seven. He had a stocky build and unruly gray hair that made him look older than he was. Jack noted that Lou's face was a little more round than when he saw him last. Looked like he had picked up a few pounds.

"You all know Lou Cros?" Captain Smitters asked.

"Yes, sir," Jack said. "How've you been, Lou?"

"Good, Jack, and you?"

"No problems. Life is good," Jack said.

"You found that special lady yet?"

"No, not yet."

"Hi, Lou," Dave chimed in.

"We're looking good, Dave. How are Rose and the family?"

"Everyone is well."

Captain Smitters cleared his throat and interrupted the conversation.

"I'm sure by now you may have heard that Lou might be heading up the investigation on the downtown homicides. This is an official notice that he will be the primary investigator. Any information you have will be shared with Lou, and in return he will keep you informed. So we don't have any missed information, Lou will have access to your daily reports. All of you will keep me informed as to the progress in this case. Any questions?" asked Captain Smitters as he looked at each man.

"No, sir," both Jack and Dave replied.

"Good. Anything to report from last night?" Captain Smitters asked.

"No problems," said Dave, who wanted to keep the conversation light. "Just an escapee from the Union Avenue Mission. Captured and returned."

Jack felt himself tighten up.

Captain Smitters forced a smile. "I'm sure I will read all about it in your report. That's all I have. You two get home and get some rest."

Jack and Dave left the captain's office and stopped by the coffeepot.

"How long have you known Lou?" Dave asked.

"Well, let's see. I graduated in criminology at the University of Memphis in 1982 and then entered the police academy the same year. I met him shortly after that. We actually worked together on some cases in the eighties. I know he was an all-state defensive guard in high school, and that he attended Middle Tennessee State University in Murfreesboro, where he graduated with a bachelor of science degree in criminal justice. He moved to Memphis and entered the police academy. Later, he was promoted to investigator and was named West Tennessee Investigator of the Year. He told me he fell in love with the city and became quite a historian. I'm glad to see him back. How does he know your wife?"

"Rose and I met him at one of the office functions back in 2003, the same year you and I partnered up. I can't believe he remembered her name."

Dave took a sip of his coffee and continued. "I'm having a problem with the case. Why would anyone want to kill a couple of homeless people? What could possibly be the motive?"

"If these two murders are related, and it sounds like they may be, we have a serial killer on the streets. A serial killer's motives are usually emotional or sexual. I'm glad Lou is on the case. If there's a link, he'll find it."

CHAPTER 2

The Ghosts of Cotton Row

Lou Cros sat patiently outside the Union Avenue Burger King. He checked the instrument panel on his 2005 dark blue Taurus. Heat waves dissipated off the black asphalt driveway. The June heat had hit with a vengeance. Thinking it would keep the car from overheating, he rolled the two front windows down and shut off the engine. He inhaled the sticky humid air as it wafted into the car. As if by some magic spell, his white shirt immediately felt clammy against his skin. Looking for his partner, Lou scanned the inside of the Burger King. It was only eleven in the morning, and already his partner, Sue Nash, had made three pit stops. *Women can't hold their coffee,* he thought. Lou watched as Sue exited the building and approached the car. Her slender, five-foot-eight-inch body seemed to glide over the black asphalt. She was smiling her usual funny smile, the one Lou recognized.

"Okay, what's up?" Lou asked.

"How'd you know something's up?"

"You have that look, like you know something I don't," he answered.

"Well, as a matter of fact, you will be glad to know that Glitter is in there, sitting in the back booth."

"Did he see you?"

"Of course not," Sue replied.

"Good. Wait here and watch the front door, in case he decides to leave before I can reach him. I'll be back in a minute."

"You think he might know something?"

"He's been pretty straight with me in the past. If there's any information on the street, he knows it."

Lou took a leisurely stroll around the parking lot and entered the Burger King through the side door. Glitter was sitting with his back against the side wall of the booth, with his legs stretched out on the seat. His feet dangled off the edge. He had gold rings on every finger, several gold bracelets, and gold chains around his neck. Sitting across from him was a young white male. As Lou approached, Glitter moved his sunglasses down the bridge of his nose and peered over the black frames.

"Lou, my man. What's up?" asked Glitter.

Lou slid into the booth across from Glitter and pinned the young white male against the wall.

"Nice outfit," Lou said.

Glitter was wearing an open-collar black silk shirt and a pair of neatly creased dark gray cuffed pants, which accented his tall, slim body. Highly polished black and brown loafers covered his feet. The two-tone colors gave them a chic European look. Lou figured him to be in his early forties. He had a short black Afro haircut and a newly grown goatee. Glitter held out a closed fist that required a knuckle touch instead of a handshake. His grin exposed a diamond embedded in a front gold tooth.

"Long time no see. What brings you out?" Glitter said.

"Just a visit with an old friend," Lou said with a laugh.

"Yeah, well, let my man out so we can discuss," Glitter said.

Lou took a good look at the young kid in the booth, committing his face to memory. "You're hanging out with bad company, kid," Lou said.

"Now, Lou, is that any way to talk to my customers? Man here just wants to buy a nice bracelet for his girl. You know my brother and I run a legit business. We've had John's Pawnshop on Madison Avenue for over twenty years. Gold is our specialty."

Lou slid out, and the kid quickly left.

"Just get a receipt," Lou shouted to the kid.

"Get a receipt! What you think, I got a secretary following me around?" laughed Glitter.

Glitter lifted one of his gold chains from around his neck. It had a six-inch *G* hanging off the end.

"How do you like my latest creation? You know I've designed some pretty fancy stuff for some famous people. Isaac Hayes, Elvis Presley, B.B. King, and Jerry Lee Lewis all wore one of my designs. You'd look good with one of these. I'll put a big *L* on there. The ladies will be all over you," Glitter said with a grin.

"Not buying. Just looking for some answers."

"Not buying! Man, you're wasting my time and taking up my booth. If you want answers, sounds to me like you're buying."

"I'm sure you already know that last week there were two homicides. Two homeless guys. You knew Skipper, right? The night he was killed, did he get caught up in something he shouldn't have?" asked Lou, ignoring Glitter's last statement.

"Why didn't you tell me this was about Skipper? Terrible thing happened to him. He was a friend of mine. Brought me customers from time to time. I took good care of him. Whoever did him in needs to be off the streets. Bad for business, you know. He never hurt anybody. Never got involved in any of that stuff. Sounds to me like somebody is making a point."

"Making a point? What do you mean?"

"You know. Making a point."

"No, I don't know. What point is someone making?" Lou asked.

"Street people. Somebody making a point about street people. Now, you're holding up my business," Glitter said, nodding toward a couple of guys standing outside the glass door. "Play safe, man. Stop by the shop anytime, and I'll give you a fitting for that chain." Glitter held his fist out again to indicate the conversation was over.

"I'll do that. Buy yourself a coke." Lou dropped a twenty on the table, touched knuckles with Glitter, and slid out of the booth.

Lou checked over the parking lot before he got back in the car. Sue was reading the morning newspaper that Lou had left on the front seat.

"Did you see what they're calling this case? The Beale Street Homicides. That must have made the mayor crazy. Any news from Glitter?" asked Sue.

"Not really. He said something that made some sense for once. He said that maybe someone was making a point about street people. We could be looking for someone who had a run-in or a bad experience with a homeless person, causing the perpetrator to snap. It could even be a street person who got hold of a gun. Maybe the perpetrator was victimized by one of his or her own. There are a lot of possibilities. We need to start looking over all reports that deal with the homeless. Maybe something will open up."

"Piece of gum? It's your favorite kind: Big Red," Sue offered. "Why don't I start at the pawnshops in this area and see how many .38-caliber handguns have been sold or traded? Not likely to find an answer, but I might get a hit from a nervous reaction to the questioning."

"Okay, that will work for me," Lou said, taking a stick of gum from Sue and grinning. "Finally got you won over. I'll go see Jim Damos. He's retired from the Union Avenue Mission, but he might have some information. I haven't seen him or Esther for quite a while. You want to meet up later tonight at the Peabody Hotel, say around 6:00 PM? We can meet in the piano bar atrium, catch a bite to eat, and take a walk around Beale Street."

"Lou Cros, are you trying to get me out on a date again?"

Lou felt his face flush. "No date. Just a social time and an exchange of information."

"Sounds like a date to me. Sorry, I have a prior commitment. Although it does sound intriguing," Sue said, teasing Lou like she often did.

"Prior commitment! Some guy moving in on me?" Lou laughed. But he was only half joking. He wanted to hear the answer.

"No, nothing like that. Just some girlfriends getting together for a night out. Your male ego is protected."

"Barhopping party? Just be sure you take along your gun."

Lou dropped Sue off at the Evergreen Apartments. On the way over, they agreed to pursue their plan and touch base in a couple of days. Lou wanted to spend a couple of nights in the Beale Street District, looking around and checking out the people.

He watched her as she got into her white Altima. She gave him a quick smile and a wave.

Lou couldn't have asked for a better partner. He had accepted her from the start, and he always took the time to explain to her what he was thinking. He wanted her to be able to react without question, and she had learned her lessons well. He considered Sue one of the best investigators in Memphis. She was smart, read people well, and had that no-fear attitude. Lou had noticed her the day she entered the police academy. Her feisty personality and auburn hair got her the nickname of *Firecracker* among her fellow officers at the precinct. He was immediately attracted to her, but he kept his professionalism intact at all times. Lou had watched her determination over the nine years she served as a police officer, pursued her master's degree, and got a promotion to investigator. He felt she had that special type of charisma and self-confidence that set people at ease.

Lou had partnered up with Sue on their first high-profile case in 1985. A body had been discovered at the Gayoso Bayou Pumping Station on Saffarans. The old bayou was a drainage canal that ran along the eastern side of the city and ended at the Wolf River. Concrete walls and ceilings were later added before the canal was buried under Danny Thomas Boulevard.

Lou was able to identify the victim as Charles "Bubba" Graves, a middle-aged white male who was the original owner of the Thunderbird Lounge. Lou had been to the lounge several times, and he enjoyed the piano playing of a young blind man named Ronnie Millsap. Bubba was a large, bearded Kentucky mountain man, whom Lou had always thought resembled the TV actor who played Grizzly Adams. In spite of his intimidating size, Bubba was a backslapping gentle man who would give away the store. The story Lou had heard on the street was that Bubba's financial backing came from a Kentucky loan shark. The debt and interest became more than the lounge was able to pay, leaving Bubba with no option other than to close the doors and walk away. That was not what his loan officer wanted to hear.

Ballistics identified the bullets as 9 mm with the unusual hexagonal right-handed barrel rifling. Lou was amazed at Sue's creative investigating. With the help of York Arms Sporting Goods in Memphis, she had figured that the gun was most likely a Glock handgun distributed by only one gun store in Louisville, Kentucky. Her pit bull investigating and attention to detail led to the arrest and conviction of Bubba's killer.

After Lou dropped Sue off, he made his way from the midtown apartments to Whitehaven. He pulled off Elvis Presley Boulevard and found Janis Drive. As he made the first curve, Lou turned into the first driveway on the right. Jim Damos's wife, Esther, an elderly black woman, peeked out the window. The front door opened; Jim stepped out onto the concrete porch and waved Lou in.

"Hey, Lou, it worried me when I got your call. Has something happened at the mission?" asked Jim.

"No, everything is good there. Just wanted to talk to you about some of the patrons," answered Lou.

"Patrons? I've heard those people called a lot of things, but never a patron." Jim chuckled. "Come on in. Esther just made some good iced tea. Have a seat."

Jim Damos was a tall, slender black man. He had a small well-groomed white mustache, high cheekbones, and short salt-and-pepper hair.

"Esther," Jim yelled, "bring Detective Cros and me a cold iced tea, please."

Jim sat down in a cloth-covered rocker. An open Bible covered the top of a small table next to the plaster walls. There were several spots of missing plaster and visible streaks of water damage on the outside wall. A worn, dusty-looking rug partially covered the wood floor. A small gas floor heater vent connected the front room to the dining area. The painted fireplace was draped in white linen, signifying that it wasn't working. Photos stretched along the mantel.

"Are those your kids and grandkids?" Lou motioned toward the fireplace.

"Yep. My two sons are on the end there, with their families. My daughter and her husband are the ones in the third picture. All the rest are grandkids. Got eleven of them. I've been very blessed. How about you? How many you got?"

"Never married. Still looking for the right one," Lou said with a grin.

"Well, you better hurry up. That gray hair is catching up with you." Jim pointed at Lou's hair and laughed.

Esther entered the room with two large mason jars of tea. "Here you are, Detective Cros. It's always good to see you. I haven't seen you since the police department helped out with the Thanksgiving dinner at the mission a couple of years ago. How the time flies. Jim says he misses the mission and seeing all his old friends. How've you been?"

"Very good, Esther. Please call me Lou. And may I say you look especially nice today. Did you do something with your hair?"

Esther touched her hair and grinned. "No, but thank you for saying so." She nudged Jim's arm. "You could learn something from this man. I'll leave you two alone. Good to see you, Detective Cros."

"You too, Esther, and it's Lou."

"Oh yeah, please excuse me. Come back anytime," she said as she left the room.

Jim flicked his wrist several times, signaling to Esther that she needed to move on. As soon as they were alone, Jim opened up the conversation.

"I'm glad you didn't say anything about the downtown murders. Esther gets scared easy, and I've been trying to keep the news from her. Only one white lady left on this street. All the other whites have moved out. There've been a couple of break-ins on the other side of the street. I'd like to move out of this area myself, but with our social security, I don't think we can. I'm hoping one of my kids will hit it big and ask old mom and dad to move into their new house. Can't ever tell. I stop by Golden Nugget Casino every week and drop me a few quarters into that Mega machine. Maybe I'll hit that million dollars one day."

"I'm sure everything will work out for the best. I know the police department has stepped up patrolling this area. Probably one of the safest areas in Whitehaven. I'm sure you and Esther will be fine. And if you hit that Mega machine, just invite me to the moving-out party," Lou said.

"I'll do that."

The two men raised their mason jars and clinked them together.

"So, what's up, Lou? What can I help you with?" Jim asked.

"The fellow who was killed by the river. Ever see him around the mission?" Lou handed Jim a picture of the victim.

"Yeah, I remember him. Never would tell me his name. Never came into the mission. I talked with him several times outside the front door. I gave him a ham sandwich once, but I couldn't get him to come inside. Didn't talk much, but he always seemed to listen. Said he had no family. He wouldn't tell me where he was from or where he was going. I figured he was passing through when he found out about the Memphis in May barbeque competition. Good way to get fed. I don't know where he stayed at night, but it wasn't at the mission," Jim said.

"Did you ever see anyone hassle him or take special notice of him?"

"You know, I saw him one night when I was leaving. I was going to get me some barbeque, and—"

"What time was that?"

"Oh, around ten. It was a Friday night, and I got off at ten. I saw a group of young white kids yelling at him about something, and one of them pushed him. The others laughed and cursed him. Called him a drunk. I turned around to see if I could help him, but he took off into the crowd. I never saw him again. Just figured he probably asked for a handout, and the kids thought they would have some fun," Jim said.

"Showing up dead isn't having fun. Did you remember anything different about the guy who pushed him?"

"No, not much. They all look the same to me," he laughed. "Just a bunch of kids. Spiked hair. Colored hair. Rings in their faces."

"You remember what color hair?" asked Lou.

"Green. Spiked and green. A real masterpiece this guy was."

"Did you ever see him after that night?" Lou asked.

"No, that was the only time. I always feel humbled when I'm around the homeless. The mission was a real calling for me. I worked there for twenty-two years. Helped a lot of people. But there's always that one you can't help. That one who won't open up. Something in his life took away his spirit. The drugs and the booze you can fix, but take away a person's spirit and he's broken. Broken people are hard to fix. Only God can do that." Jim motioned toward the open Bible. "Psalm 34:19 reminds us, 'The Lord is close to the brokenhearted; He rescues those who are crushed in spirit.'"

"Thanks, Jim. You've been more help than you know. If anything else comes to mind, give me a call. Do you have one of my cards?"

"Oh yeah. Carry it with me." Jim grinned as he patted his wallet.

Lou turned up the mason jar and finished his tea. "Thanks for the tea, Esther," he shouted into the back room.

"You're welcome," she responded from the next room.

"Take care, Jim. Keep in touch."

"You too."

Lou pulled out of Jim and Esther's driveway and headed downtown. It was almost five, and with the Memphis evening traffic, it took almost an hour before he reached his destination. He pulled into the parking garage next to the South Second Street alley. The smell of the Rendezvous' barbeque permeated the evening air. The streets were starting to fill up with people. There was already a small line outside the restaurant door that stretched into the alley. Lou passed through the alley and crossed the street. As he entered the Peabody Hotel, he passed the retail stores, found a seat by the piano bar, and ordered a Bacardi and Coke. He closed his eyes and let his mind drift. His thoughts were pulled to Sue.

He saw her coming into the hotel. She was dressed in a round-neck white dress and white high heels. White pearls adorned her neckline. Her hair was curled under on the ends. She walked elegantly across the tapestry-style rug and sat down at the bar. A businessman in a gray suit approached her. They exchanged a few words, and he left. Lou got up and walked toward her. She saw him and smiled. He offered her his hand, and she took it. He led her to an open space on the dance floor and pressed her close to him as they started dancing. Her hair tickled his face.

"Another drink, sir?"

Lou was so lost in thought that he almost jumped out of his chair.

"Would you like another drink?" the waitress asked again.

"Oh, uh, no thank you. How much do I owe?" he asked, feeling a little embarrassed.

"That'll be five fifty," she said.

Lou paid the waitress, but he remained seated for a while longer and listened to the piano music. After several questioning looks from the waitress, he headed to the Beale Street District. The streets were just starting to buzz with people. A group of young black men, known as the Beale Street Flippers, performed acrobatics on the brick street for tips. Music poured out of every open door. Barkers stood outside the restaurants and offered free drink coupons and a two-for-one dinner. The competition was fierce early in the evening. Lou stopped at one of the open wall beer stands and ordered a dark beer and hot dog with extra mustard. After he finished eating, Lou made several trips up and down Beale Street, working the restaurant barkers for information and showing them a picture of the Riverside victim. One barker thought he might have seen him but wasn't sure.

"I don't know, man. Maybe. Homeless people wander around here sometimes. I'm not the regular guy on the door."

"So, when will the regular guy be back?" Lou asked.

"Tomorrow. He'll be back tomorrow."

"You remember seeing any kids last week with spiked hair?"

"Man, you're asking the wrong guy. Go ask Joe over there across the street. He was here last week."

Lou crossed the street and approached the barker in front of the Blues City Café. After showing his badge and the picture of the victim, he got a hit.

"Yeah, I remember him," Joe said. "He came through here running like someone was chasing him. He ran into a guy on the street and knocked him over. Never stopped or even looked back."

"Did you see anyone?"

"No. I first thought he had picked someone's pocket, but there was nobody following him that I could tell. Maybe something scared him."

"Did you see any kids with spiked hair that night? Maybe one with green spiked hair?"

"I do remember seeing some kids with spiked hair last week. Can't really remember if any of them had green hair, though."

"What do you mean you can't remember if any of them were green? It's not like you see that every day!"

"Man, it was the last week of the May festival! The streets were packed! There were a lot of those types here last week."

Lou thanked the barker and gave him a card, saying he should call if he remembered anything else before moving on to question several more barkers. He got no new information. Walking over to South Second Street, Lou entered Huey's and ordered a beer. The waitress had jet-black hair, several face piercings, black lipstick, and purple fingernail polish.

"You ever see this guy?" he asked.

The waitress looked at the picture. "Yeah, he was hanging around outside last week. Asking customers for money. Boss had to run him off."

"Is your boss here?"

"You a cop or something?"

"Investigator."

"Got some ID?" the waitress asked.

"Do I need ID to talk to your boss?"

"No, just wanted to see it. Hey, Jimmy, cop out here wants to see you," she shouted, causing all the customers to stop talking and look over at Lou.

"Thanks, uh, miss?"

"Don't mention it," she laughed. "Name's Kat. Need something, call me."

A balding middle-aged man wandered out from the back. Approaching Lou's table, he wiped his hands on a less-than-white apron.

"What can I do for you?" the manager asked.

"Name is Lou Cros. I'm investigating the Riverside murder last week. You remember this guy?" Lou handed him the victim's picture.

"Yeah, he was harassing my customers. I told him to get lost."

"Anything else?"

"Nope. Just ran him off," the manager replied.

"Did you happen to see some young kids on the same night? One with green spiked hair?"

"Yeah, they were in here. They got a big laugh out of it. Left right afterward. Kind of a mean streak in the green-haired guy. Gave Kat a hard time."

"Ever see him before?" inquired Lou.

"Yeah, I see him around from time to time. Had a few words with him that night. He stopped coming in."

"You remember what it was about?"

"He was hitting on Kat. She didn't like it. That was about it."

"Know his name?"

"No, but Kat probably does. Hey, Kat, your turn again," the manager yelled across the bar. "Need me anymore? Got things to do."

"No, that's it." Lou handed him one of his cards. "If you see him again, give me a call."

"Yeah, sure."

Kat took her time getting back over to the table. "Need another beer?" she asked.

"In a minute. Your boss says there was a group of guys in here the night you were talking about. Guy with spiked green hair. You know him?"

"No, just a creep showing off in front of his friends," she replied.

"You remember them calling his name?"

"Yeah, they called him Boots or Bootie or something like that. Real creepy guy. Jimmy had to ask him to leave."

Lou placed his card and a ten-dollar bill on the table. "If you see him again, give me a call. I'll skip the beer."

"Sure."

Lou drank the rest of his beer and then headed down to Front Street. He was feeling light-headed. He needed to get away from the loud music and street noise. He turned north toward the Convention Center, crossed the street, and climbed the winding concrete steps to the walkover monorail bridge that spanned the Mississippi River to Mud Island. From the bridge, he could see the thirty-two-story stainless-steel Arena Pyramid that sat on the bank of the river. The lights on the bridge reflected small moon-shaped dots into the water below. The concrete walkway vibrated as the monorail passed under the Mud Island Bridge and made another trip to the museum.

The night air felt damp against his skin. He felt his heart race for a moment and then slow down. He had never been a heavy drinker, but in the past year he found himself hitting the bottle more often. He took out the bottle of aspirin that he always carried, dumped three tablets onto the palm of his right hand, and swallowed the tablets dry. He felt his hand tremble as he wiped sweat off his face. Lou climbed back down the steps and headed back toward Beale Street to get his car. As he walked along the west side of the street overlooking the river, he stopped at Confederate Park. Leaning on the old stone wall, he watched a tugboat push a coal barge through the choppy brown water, and then he looked across the street. On the corner of Jefferson and Front was a four-story office building. For almost sixty years, the one hundred-fifty-room King Cotton Hotel had stood on that site, until the building was demolished in 1984. As he left the park, Lou walked along the abandoned Cotton Row Warehouse District. Night shadows spread through the street.

All of a sudden, Lou felt dizzy and cold. His vision blurred. His mind began to spin out of control. His heart raced. A sharp pain sparked in his head and ran down his back into both legs. Perspiration covered his face and soaked into his clothes. Ghostly visions of cotton merchants started to appear from thin air, as they walked through the deteriorating brick walls. Black porters with spiny skeletal hands pushed huge bales of cotton on wood dollies from one warehouse to another. Lou lowered his head and avoided eye contact with the black empty sockets that stared off into space. Quickening his pace, he walked among the ghosts. Their days were long past, gone long ago like the Cotton Carnival and steamboats.

Once Lou broke free from the shadows, the visions disappeared. He rested his back against the side of a brick building and took a deep breath. Slowly, the pounding in his chest subsided, and his anxiety passed. As he moved toward Beale Street, he saw a few tourists talking and laughing as they made their way along the sidewalk. The rest of the night was blurred with beer, people, and loud music. He headed home around midnight.

The ring of his cell phone jarred Lou awake. He glanced at his alarm clock radio. Six forty-five. He fumbled around on his nightstand before he realized the phone was in his coat pocket. He was fully dressed, having fallen asleep in his clothes.

"Lou, Captain Smitters. We have another homicide. Same MO. We're at the old Firestone tire plant at Firestone and Manassas. How soon can you be here?"

"Fifteen minutes. Tops." Lou rubbed his eyes. "I'm on my way."

Lou walked into the bathroom and splashed water on his face. He felt terrible. He squirted some toothpaste on his toothbrush and began to brush his teeth, trying to brush away the dry rancid taste in his mouth. He let some water run over his hands, and then he passed his wet fingers through his hair before hurrying out the door. He couldn't remember when he had driven home or had gotten into bed. His head pounded. He chewed three aspirin and forced them down. The bottle was almost empty. He made a mental note to pick another one up on the way home.

With yesterday's conversations running through his mind, he made it to the Firestone plant in record time. Several police cars were on the street. Yellow security tape blocked a door on the Firestone Avenue entrance. He spotted Captain Smitters standing outside talking with an officer. The captain looked up as Lou approached. He had an "I can't believe what I'm seeing" look on his face. Captain Smitters blasted Lou for his appearance.

"Tuck in your shirt and straighten your tie, Cros. Press could be here at any moment. You look like hell. Did you sleep in your clothes?"

"As a matter of fact, I did."

The captain frowned but ignored Lou's comment. "Doc's inside along with the crime scene unit. Fellow in the car over there found the victim about thirty minutes ago."

"Are you taking him downtown?" Lou asked.

"Not sure where we're taking him. I'll make some phone calls. Homeless guy. Said the victim was living inside the building. Stopped by to check on him. Found him dead. You want to talk to him before we take him?" the captain inquired.

"Sure. Let me see the doc first."

Lou crossed the tapeline. The entry door's padlock and hasp were broken, and the doorknob was hanging on by a piece of duct tape. Dusting powder was smeared on the doorframe. An extension cord ran inside the building from a generator on the back lip of the CSU vehicle. A floor lamp was set up inside the door, and another one was set up outside an office in the hallway. An officer inside recognized Lou and let him pass.

Lou stopped outside the office. Tape was stretched across its entrance. More dusting powder appeared on the metal-framed entryway. The dust-ridden floor had been wiped, removing any footprints that might have been there. The medical examiner was bent over a body. The room was a typical office, about ten by ten with no door, just the metal-framed entryway. The linoleum floor was covered with old clothes, trash, and newspapers. In one corner, Lou could see several candles under a handmade clothes hanger stand that supported a small pot. Corrugated boxes were stacked in the far corner.

The corpse was sprawled out on top of them. Splattered blood stained the back wall to a height of about three feet.

"Hi, Doc. Where's the rest of the CSU?" Lou asked.

The examiner didn't turn around, but he recognized Lou's voice. "They wanted to check out the building for any other entry points. I wouldn't cross over yet until they clear you for the scene."

"What do you have?" Lou inquired.

"White male, early fifties. One bullet entry left frontal skull area. Exited the occipital bone near the lambdoidal suture," the examiner said.

"English, please."

"He got shot in the front of the head, and the bullet came out lower than the entry on the back side. He was sitting here, and whoever shot him was standing up. From the temperature reading, I'd say the time of death was around 2:00 AM."

"Thanks, Doc. Now that wasn't so hard, was it?" joked Lou.

The ME laughed and finally turned around to face Lou. He had that same surprised look on his face as Captain Smitters. "Lou, are you feeling all right? Your face looks flushed."

Lou tried to straighten his shirt the best he could, and he ran his fingers through his hair again. "Out late. Ate something that didn't agree with me."

"Go get some rest."

"Thanks, Doc. I'll check with you later in the day."

Lou left the building. Captain Smitters was talking on his cell phone, probably to the mayor. Not wanting to get any of the mayor's fallout, Lou headed for the police car where the homeless man was being held. The car's back windows were partially down. As he approached the car, he understood why. Lou circled the car to stay upwind of the odor. An officer standing outside tried to hide his smile at Lou's reaction to the smell.

In the backseat was a short thin white male with a scraggly gray beard. He was wearing several shirts and a brown stocking cap. A brown hunting jacket rested across a pair of green corduroy pants. On his feet was a pair of black tennis shoes with no laces. Lou was always amazed at how the homeless could stand wearing so many clothes in the ninety-degree-plus weather. Even approaching upwind, the smell almost gagged him. Standing outside the car window, Lou introduced himself.

"My name is Lou Cros. I'm an investigator with the Memphis Police Department."

"Hello, Mr. Cros. My name is Joy Fully." The man smiled and raised his hand close to his mouth. He touched his thumb to each finger as he spoke. His voice was high-pitched and a little squeaky. "It certainly looks like a nice day. Don't you agree, Mr. Cros?" He continued to touch his fingers as he spoke.

"Yes, it is indeed going to be a nice day. May I call you Joy?"

"Oh yes, that would be splendid. All my friends call me Joy. Can we be friends, Mr. Cros?"

"Yes, we can be friends," Lou replied.

Joy gave a little bounce off the seat. "Wonderful!"

"Was the man inside a friend of yours?"

"Oh yes. Pat was a very good friend. Terrible thing that happened to him. I don't know why anyone would want to hurt Pat. Why, I've seen him pick up little spiders and take them outside to set them free. He loved all of God's little creatures." His hand movements continued.

"He sounds like he was a very good man," Lou stated.

"Oh my, yes. He was my best friend. Sometimes, he would share his dinner with me. I knew he didn't have enough. But Pat—he wouldn't have it any other way. Do you know who hurt him?"

"No, but I am going to find out. Do you want to help me?"

"Oh my, yes. That would be splendid." Joy bounced on the seat again.

"Can you tell me how you found him?" asked Lou.

"Well, I haven't seen Pat for a while and wanted to stop by to see him. So, I came by to see him. I came in and called for him. He didn't answer, so I turned on my flashlight and went to his room. They will give me my flashlight back, won't they, Mr. Cros?"

"Yes, I will see that you get your flashlight back. So, you went inside, and then what?"

"Well, there he was," continued Joy. "He was just staring at the ceiling. He looked so sad. It upset me very much." The smile disappeared from his face, and his fingers stopped moving.

"Did you see or hear anything?" asked Lou.

"No, it was very quiet and very sad."

"Did you touch anything?" Lou's probing continued.

"No, I was just very sad."

"What did you do next?"

"I went back outside with my flashlight and waited until that nice officer came by. He took my flashlight. I will get my flashlight back, won't I, Mr. Cros?"

"Yes, Joy, you'll get it back."

"Oh, that will be splendid." Joy bounced on the car seat and started to drum his fingers again. "Why would anyone want to hurt Pat, Mr. Cros?"

"There are some strange people in this world, Joy."

Joy laughed and bounced on the seat. "Oh my, yes. There sure are."

"Did you ever see anyone push Pat around or treat him badly?" asked Lou.

"Oh no, Mr. Cros. I've seen Pat pick up little spiders and put them outside to set them free. He loved all of God's little creatures."

"Have you ever seen a young man with green-colored spiked hair in this area?"

"Oh my, no," laughed Joy. "That would look very silly. I will get my flashlight back, won't I, Mr. Cros?"

"Yes, Joy. You will get your flashlight back. Thank you for your help."

"You are so welcome, Mr. Cros. I hope we can talk again. It is going to be a beautiful day."

One of the officers approached the car. "Captain wants to see you."

The captain met Lou halfway and started right in.

"I need you to do whatever it takes to get this case moving. This is your baby 24/7. You let me know if you need any more help. Anything I can do right now?" asked the captain.

"I would like to get a BOLO out for a young white male. Early twenties. Medium height and build. He has green spiked hair and several facial piercings. Probably has a gothic look. Hangs out around the Beale Street District."

"May not need to. Picked up a kid like that last night. Drunk and disorderly. Picked him up in Overton Square. He's been in the drunk tank overnight."

"Give them a call and hold on to him until I can get there. He's the only suspect we have at this time."

"I'll take care of it. What else?" the captain inquired.

"What's going to happen to him?" Lou gestured toward the police car.

"Harmless enough. We'll take him to the Memphis Mental Health Center. They agreed to take him in for a couple of days and do an evaluation. See if they can find some relatives. I want to get as many homeless people off the street as I can."

"Look, Captain, you mind if I give him a pin light? He is worried sick about his flashlight."

"No, I don't see any harm in that," replied the captain, with a questioning look on his face.

Lou returned to his car and searched his glove box. Finding the pin light, he returned to the police car and handed it to Joy.

"If you push the silver button on the end, a light will come on."

"Oh my, this is splendid! Mr. Cros, how did you make it so small? This is just splendid!" Pushing the button on the light, he shined it against the back of the front seat. "Just splendid!"

Lou hurried to his car to meet up with the green-haired monster. On his way to the station, he called Sue and filled her in on the latest homicide. She agreed to meet him at the station and bring him up-to-date on her pawnshop investigation. Briefly, only one shop clerk showed some nervousness over the questioning. Could be a lead, she said.

CHAPTER 3

The Soothsayer

LOU SAT IN THE interrogation room with his back facing the two-way mirror. While Sue stood on the other side of the mirror, ready to listen to the interrogation through the speaker mounted on the wall, Lou scanned the file folder: Randolph Booth, age twenty-three, address was 816 Avalon, apartment 3C. Two priors, both juvenile, for assault with a deadly weapon. Seemed that he had beaten two other kids with a baseball bat. Received one-year probation, with paying compensation and doing some community service. One DUI last year, fined, nine-month suspended license, and ninety-day weekend duty at a rehab unit.

An officer entered the room with Booth and motioned for the young man to take a seat at the table across from Lou. Closing the door, the officer remained inside, guarding against an unexpected exit. The young man slouched in the chair, crossed his arms, and stared defiantly at Lou. His posture said, "You'll get nothing out of me." Lou welcomed the challenge. He leaned forward in his seat to get into as much of the kid's space as he could.

"Nice hairdo. What do you call that?"

Booth continued to stare and gave no reply.

"Name is Cros, with one *S*. I want to remind you that you were read your rights when you were brought in on the drunk and disorderly charges. Got any questions?"

The kid stared straight ahead.

"Good."

Lou looked at the folder again. "Pretty nice little rap sheet you're building for yourself, Mr. Booth. A couple of assaults and a DUI. I just have a few questions for you, and then you can go. I was by Huey's downtown this week, and lo and behold, your name came up. Seems like you got in a little pissing match with a waitress and the manager. Then, a couple of witnesses saw you do a little job on a homeless man outside the restaurant. Just thought you might remember this guy."

Lou took the picture out and pushed it across the table. The green-haired kid glanced down but showed no sign of interest.

"Seems that very night, someone put a bullet in his head. You know anything about that?"

"Hey, what the hell is this? I'm here on a drunk and disorderly charge. I don't have to answer your questions. You can't hold me. I want a lawyer," he demanded.

Lou looked over at the officer. "Would you mind getting me a bottle of water while I explain Mr. Booth's rights to him again? I'll take full responsibility. We're okay here. You can lock the door on the outside when you leave."

The officer left the room. Booth slouched down in the chair and made a disgusting sound with his lips.

"You're partially right, Mr. Booth. I can't hold you on a drunk and disorderly charge, but you'll need to stay here until you make bail. Could take another day to get in front of a judge. Maybe longer. But let me tell you what I can do. I can get you rearrested for assault and suspicion of murder. I can make it happen in a couple of hours. So, we can do it easy, or we can do it hard. You want a lawyer? We can get you a lawyer. But unless you have a lawyer on retainer, you'll have to wait until we reach the public defender's office. You'll probably miss your lunch and be here all day. Or, you can answer me a few questions and probably be on your way by noon."

"That's blackmail! You can't get away with this!"

Ignoring the outburst, Lou continued. "What kind of work do you do, Mr. Booth?"

"Web design. I do Web designs."

"At home or in an office?"

"At home."

"You own a gun, Mr. Booth?"

"No!"

"If I get a search warrant for your apartment, are we going to find anything unusual?"

"I'm through answering your questions! I want a lawyer!"

"Fine. We're all done. We just have to wait for the officer."

Lou drummed his fingers on the table. The kid wiped a bead of sweat from his face.

"Your spikes are drooping," Lou said, barely suppressing a smirk.

The kid jumped up and kicked his chair over just as the officer came into the room.

"What the—?" The officer placed his hand on his gun.

"We're okay, Officer," Lou said. "Mr. Booth is just a little excited."

The officer relaxed his stance. He was holding the bottle of water Lou had asked for. He set the bottle on the table. Lou leaned back in his chair and grinned. Making a quick address note, he closed the folder and handed it to the officer.

"I'll be seeing you real soon, Mr. Booth," Lou said.

Once the officer led Randolph Booth from the room, Lou checked the adjacent room for Sue. It was empty. Looking through the front glass door, he saw her sitting in his car.

"How'd you get in my car?"

"Wasn't locked," Sue replied.

"Did you hear the questioning?"

"Yeah, I did. He got pretty nervous when you asked about searching his apartment. He'll be looking for you. I can set up a little stakeout at his house for the rest of the day and see if anybody shows up. We need to know when and where he goes."

"Perfect. What about the pawnshops?"

"Not much to report on the shops. Guy at South Memphis Pawn on Third Street showed some uneasy body language when I showed the picture of the Riverside victim and asked about his records on any .38-caliber handguns. I think he's hiding something. Name is Gary West. He's an overweight white guy with a beard and a Mohawk haircut. Has a skull and crossbones tattooed on his right forearm. I don't think you will have any trouble finding him. Says he works nights from eleven to eleven. Probably selling out the back door for cash."

"The captain is on me pretty hard for any information," Lou said. "If you handle the green-haired kid today, I'll make some more stops and hang out on Beale Street tonight. Give me a call if Booth takes off with some of his buddies. Maybe I can check out his apartment when he leaves."

"I didn't hear that. You're the one who's going to get busted if you keep going around procedure."

"Oh yeah, right. I never said that." Lou smiled.

Boots stepped outside the station and pushed speed dial No. 1 on his cell phone.

"Come on, pick up."

"What's up, Boots?" said the person who answered.

"I got busted last night. I need you to pick me up at the police station on Union Avenue. My car is over in Overton Square," Boots said.

"What's going on?"

"Nothing major. Some scumbag got smart with the wrong guy. I had to rearrange his nose. Place called the cops."

"Man, I hate I missed that," the voice said, and laughed.

"Wait a minute," continued Boots. "There's a detective here giving me a hard time. I'm pretty sure someone is waiting to see who picks me up. Never mind about coming to get me. I'll call a cab."

"So, what's going on?"

"You remember that homeless guy we pushed around at Huey's? Well, seems someone put a bullet through his head that night. When I left that night, you guys were still partying pretty heavy. You know anything about the bum?"

Silence.

"Tell me, man! What happened?"

No reply.

"J., you better tell me. This dick is not going to go away."

"Nothing happened, Boots. I swear! We didn't do anything. We never saw him again."

"You better not be lying to me, J."

"Nothing, man, I swear. Did you tell him our names?"

"No way. Didn't tell him anything. Got to go. I'll call you tomorrow. We need to move the stuff from here to your place. I get the feeling that this guy is going to be snooping around."

"We can do that. What do want me to do?" asked J.

"I'd like to set things up in your basement. We can put a padlock on the door and paint the windows black or cover them with something," Boots said.

"Okay, call me when you're ready."

"When you come, be sure there's no pig tail on you. Drive around the block several times and pay attention to any cars you see. If something looks even a little weird, keep going. You got that?"

"Sure, Boots. I understand."

"And, J., when you pull in, drive around to the back of the apartment. Sit there until I motion you in."

"Will do."

Boots closed his phone. Feeling nervous, he returned to the station and approached the front counter. An officer talking on the phone sat behind the counter at a desk. His shirtsleeves looked like they were cutting the circulation off from his massive arms. The officer hung up and made a notation on a yellow pad.

"I need a cab. Where's your phone book?" Boots asked.

The officer held up his hand as the desk phone rang.

"Memphis Police Department. Fifth Precinct. Sergeant Neely speaking."

Boots waited as Sergeant Neely responded with a yes and no and hung up. He picked up his pen and started jotting down information on the yellow pad again.

"I need a phone number for a cab," Boots insisted.

The sergeant never looked up, but he reached inside a desk drawer and pulled out a phone book. He placed the book on the counter. "Don't leave this area," he muttered.

Boots quickly got the number of a cab company, deliberately left the phone book just outside of the officer's reach, and headed for the front door. He could see the sergeant's reflection in the window glass as he got up out of his chair and mumbled something to himself.

"Have a good day, Officer," Boots shouted over his shoulder and pushed through the front door. A yellow cab pulled up several minutes later. Boots gave the driver his address and leaned back in the seat and closed his eyes.

Since Sue was going to handle Boots, Lou decided to travel back to the Firestone plant. He wanted to see if he could scrape up any witnesses at the projects along Manassas. Most of the drug pushers sold their candy at night. Maybe someone had seen something.

Turning on Manassas off of Chelsea Avenue, Lou slowed down to carefully survey the area. The scarred red brick projects appeared on his left. White graffiti covered the end building at its base. A broken washing machine sat on the brown dirt lawn alongside a concrete walk. Plywood boarded windows, and metal grate storm doors filled most of the spotty-white effervescence-stained brick openings, caused from the high alkaline mortar mix that was never acid cleaned. Box fans and several air conditioners extended out of the other openings as they strained to cool the humid Memphis air. A broken metal chair leaned against a rotting porch support column. Broken plastic toys appeared to push up through the brown dirt like spots of weeds.

An older model dark blue Cadillac was parked at the last building on the wrong side of the street. The license plate read Big John. A white male with a goatee sat on its hood. He was smoking a cigarette, and he was wearing blue jeans and a sleeveless T-shirt. The sun flashed off his neck chain cross. John Fagan was well known by Lou and the Memphis Police Department.

Lou pulled up to the curb next to the old Weyerhaeuser box plant that was once Mead Container. There were bullet holes in the plant windows along the railroad track side of the building, and in the day it wasn't uncommon for cars to be stolen right out of the plant parking lot. The area became so infested with crime and violence that Weyerhaeuser shut its Memphis plant down in 1995 and moved it to Olive Branch, Mississippi. From his vantage point, Lou could see the yellow tape that crossed the door at the Firestone plant. One police car still remained in the front parking lot. Lou's head began to throb. He grabbed his last three aspirin tablets, tossed them into his mouth, took a deep breath, and exited the car. Big John took the last drag off his cigarette and flicked it into the street. As Lou approached, John took out another cigarette. He glanced at Lou as he flicked open his lighter.

"Hey, John."

John took a deep drag but didn't respond. Even with John sitting on the car's hood, Lou still looked up at him. Big John wore the scars of gang battles across his face and arms.

Lou asked, "What's with the cop car over there?" Lou knew it was a stupid question, but Big John wasn't the brightest bulb on the tree. Stupid and Big John went quite well together, and Lou figured that a stupid question might just get the man talking.

John took another drag off his cigarette and tried to stare Lou down. Lou held his stare. He knew not to break the silence. Unshaven patches of white whiskers surrounded the deep craters in John's face. A scar on his right cheek ran from the bottom of his ear to the edge of his lip, resembling a thin piece of dental floss. Several lines of scar tissue, delivered from bony knuckles or beer bottles, broke his eyebrows. Ten seconds passed. Twenty seconds. Thirty seconds.

"Somebody got snuffed, but you already knew that, didn't you, man?" John said.

Lou held back his smile.

"What brings you down here?"

Another few seconds slipped by. John flicked his second cigarette into the street.

"Business," he replied.

"What kind of business?"

"My business," John replied instantly.

"John, John, John. Why do you want to make it so hard?" Lou took out his cell phone and staged a fake call.

"Hi, Sue. Lou Cros here. Could you check to see if John Fagan has any outstanding traffic or parking tickets while I hold?"

John stood up. His six-foot six-inch, two hundred fifty-pound frame towered over Lou. Even though John was in his late sixties, he was still intimidating.

"Man here owes some money. Just here to collect it," said John.

"Never mind that check, Sue," Lou said, closing his phone. "Now, that wasn't hard, was it?"

A screen door banged on its frame. A small boy wearing only shorts ran barefoot down the cracked walkway. He ran up to John, handed him an envelope, and took off back toward the apartment. A slender black male opened the screen door as the boy disappeared into the dark entry hall. John looked into the envelope, folded it in half, and pushed it into his back pocket. The man's silhouette was watching from behind the screen door. John opened his car door and folded himself into the front seat.

"Good to see you again, John," Lou said. "Hope we can talk again another time."

Lou saw a small smile crack on Big John's face as he pulled away from the curb. As the car passed, a faint smell of burning oil permeated the humid air.

Lou remembered when Big John Fagan was once one of the most feared men in Memphis. Now he was collecting debts for chump change that probably paid for his beer and cigarettes. During the 1960s, John ran with the Tiller Clan. The clan, made up of Charles "Dago" Tiller and three cousins— George, Michael, and Albert—left behind blood and violence throughout the city. Dago Tiller died in 2004 from injures sustained in 1994, when a group of inmates beat him with softball bats at the Riverbend Maximum Security Institution in Nashville. He was serving a two-hundred-year sentence for a double homicide.

Lou had been involved in the investigation when cousin Michael dropped out of sight in 1975. Lou believed that Dago and another Tiller murdered Michael in DeSoto County, Mississippi, for being an informant. Michael's body was never found, and the indictments were dropped when one of Lou's key witnesses couldn't be located. Albert was in and out of jail most of his life and died in 2006. George Tiller was serving a ten-year federal prison sentence without parole when the clan dissolved. All of John's partners were either dead or in jail. Lou figured he would someday die as he had lived, for it was all he knew.

As if by some magical time rift, kids appeared outside the apartments. Lou walked along the sidewalk and knocked on the doors of the two closest apartments to Firestone Boulevard, but no one answered the door. The kids kept their distance and eyed him with suspicion. Lou looked back toward his car, as two middle-aged black men appeared to have some interest in it. They were leaning on the chain-link fence about twenty-five yards from his car. Lou opened his phone again and walked back toward his car. His thumb was ready to push his speed dial number to the police station. Pretending to be in a conversation, he laughed out loud. As he approached, the two men turned and slowly walked away. Since he was doing no good here, Lou decided to check in with the medical examiner. In person.

A short time later, Lou pulled into the ME's parking lot and pressed the call button on the back entry door of the office and lab. It took just a few seconds for the speaker box to react.

"Yes?"

"Hey, Doc. It's Lou Cros."

Lou heard the buzzer that unlocked the door. Dr. Paul Craft stood inside the door as a sentinel with gloved hands. Lou had met the doc twelve years earlier when he had become the medical examiner for the city of Memphis. A body lay in waiting behind him on a slightly tilted stainless-steel gurney. A strong odor of rubbing alcohol and formaldehyde filled the white-tiled room. Tools of the trade gleamed under the bright overhead lights. Motorized gadgets hung from the ceiling, while others appeared to push their way up through the floor tiles. Video cameras and microphones stood erect along the side of the stainless-steel gurneys. Lou guessed Doc to be in his late fifties, and he bore a remarkably close resemblance to the actor Paul Newman. Doc was similar in build, height, and hair color. He also possessed Newman's piercing blue eyes.

"Hey, Doc, is that the victim from the Firestone plant?"

"Yes, we got an ID. Name is Pat Romans. Has one brother living in Kansas. His brother is in the last stages of cancer. Has hospice staying with him. I hate it when someone has to identify a relative through a videoconference. He said that he hasn't seen or talked to Pat for the last five years. I asked him if they had any relatives in the Memphis area. He said they didn't. Then he started to cry and asked how much it would cost to bury him. Said he didn't have any money. Sad, isn't it?"

Paul looked at Lou and tried to change the mood. He started to pat him on the shoulder, realized his hands were gloved, and forced a smile. "I just finished my external examination," he said. "You want to hang around for the internal?"

"No, thanks. I don't think that will help me any, unless he has a camera in his stomach. Anything of note?" asked Lou.

"Not much. White male, fifty-two, five-ten, and one hundred seventy pounds. A few rat bites around his ankles, face, and the back of his head—all postmortem. I put the time of death at around 2:00 AM. There was some bruising on his arms and legs, but the color indicates it wasn't recent. I found no evidence of a struggle. The blood around the entry and exit gunshot wound indicates he was alive when he was shot. He had a lot of powder burns on his face. The killer probably was standing within a foot or two when he pulled the trigger. Could be a .38-caliber round. Ballistics will confirm later today."

"I'm always amazed at how much you guys can find out just by looking at a body."

"You have to remember that I worked with Dr. Bill Bass, one of the top forensic anthropologists in the country and founder of the Body Farm."

"I visited that place once, way back in the eighties, shortly after it opened. I have to say, it wasn't one of my favorite places. I remember it being behind the University of Tennessee Medical Center."

"That's right. I finished my graduate studies while working at the Body Farm. We had over a hundred human corpses donated each year, which were placed in different situations in order to analyze the chemical reactions of decomposition. The research data was crucial to determine the time of death. On any given day, dozens of corpses were examined and cataloged at every state of decay."

"Sounds like a wonderful life, Doc," teased Lou. "Any unusual marks on the body?"

"No, I found nothing. There were no ligature marks on the body either."

"Anything else?"

"I do have one thing that will be of interest to you. I found this card in his pocket."

Lou took the sealed plastic bag. Inside was a tattered business card from the Union Avenue Mission. Pete Johnson's name was written on the bottom left corner. A cold chill ran through Lou's body. A vision of the naked corpse was standing behind the doc. His empty eye sockets stared in Lou's direction. The vision vanished in less than a second.

"Lou, are you okay? You're white as a sheet."

"I don't know, Doc. All of the sudden, I just don't feel so well."

Lou handed the bag back to Paul and wiped sweat from his face.

"Lou, you're sweating. It's sixty degrees in here! Sit down a minute. Are you on some meds I should know about?"

"No, Doc, I'm good. Just need to get some rest."

"Sit down a minute. Let me get you some water."

"Thanks, Doc, but I have to go. If anything shows up, give me a call."

Lou quickly left via the back door. He could hear the doc yelling something at him, but couldn't make it out. Voices filled his head. For a split second, everything turned in slow motion. Entering his car, Lou grabbed the steering wheel with both hands and took a deep breath. Picking up his aspirin bottle, he threw the empty bottle against the passenger door. Starting the car, Lou turned the AC on high and pointed the vents toward his face. He sat still until he felt his muscles relax.

Parking along Riverside Drive, Lou stared at the Mississippi River and tried to get his thoughts in order. A small tugboat pushed a barge into the Wolf River Harbor. The noon sun beat down on the black rocks along the shore that were shining wet from the wake of the boat. The grassy area of land by Memphis Riverboats Inc. was filling with afternoon patrons. Joggers sounded out a rhythmic beat as their tennis shoes pounded the concrete walkway. A young man propelled a Frisbee in flight that was snatched out of the air by a black Labrador. A woman ran beside her helmet-clad daughter and struggled to keep her balanced on the leaning bike.

Lou's mind began to wander, and thoughts came and went. Lou saw himself sitting on a wood bench along the river's edge. Sue was with him. She was dressed in blue jeans and a white polo shirt. Her hair was pulled back and tied with a white sash. He had his arm on the back of the bench just inside her shoulder. She smiled, and they laughed like school kids. He felt the muscles pull on his face as he smiled and spoke her name out loud. Closing his eyes, he replayed the scene again and again. His world seemed peaceful and relaxed. He scarcely realized it, but he fell asleep.

A deep bass tugboat horn jerked Lou back to consciousness. A couple of hours had passed. His clothes felt sticky from the hot humid air. Glancing down toward the bench, he noted that new activity was taking place. His mind was clear. His thoughts were back in order. It was time to pay another visit to the mission.

Walking up Union Avenue, Lou stopped at the window of the Cotton Museum at the Memphis Cotton Exchange Building. Dated pictures and small For Sale cotton bale samples filled the storefront display. On the wall, Lou could see an old quotation board that served as a monitor of cotton pricing and market conditions. Next to it hung a plaque, which read: "The Cotton Exchange was established in 1873, and was originally located at the corner of Second and Court Avenue South."

At the next corner, Lou crossed the Main Street Trolley rail loop. Crowds of people began to build. A large group of Asian tourists blocked the Peabody Hotel windows as they lined up in groups and had their pictures taken. From the corner, Lou could see the Greyhound Bus Terminal sign. Across the street and down a few buildings was the Union Avenue Mission. Transients wandered around the area. Some carried bulging paper bags with handles. Others pulled small carts or wagons piled high with clothes and paper. Two or three just stood and stared off into space. Lou checked his watch. Lunchtime had ended at the mission, and the customers were returning to whatever they called home. A patrol car inched along the curb, and the officers inside it checked on the afternoon crowd. The car stopped.

"Hey, Lou. Are you lost?" one of the officers asked.

Lou recognized Jack Mills and Dave Drake. He walked over to them. "I'm not lost. I'm right here," Lou said with a grin.

"Are you going to be around later today?" asked Jack.

"Yes, I was planning on staying around Beale Street tonight. You guys looking for a free meal?"

"I'm always looking for a free meal," jumped in Dave. "I will gladly pay you Tuesday for a hamburger today."

"Dave is dying for a Belly Buster over at Dyer's," said Jack. "It's his favorite stopping off place. He loves their deep-fried hamburgers. Their claim is that they never change the cooking grease."

"What time do you get off?" Lou asked.

"We're heading in at four. By the time we get cleaned up and change clothes, it'll be around six. Why don't we meet you at Dyer's at six thirty?"

"Sounds good to me. I'll see you there," Lou said.

"Thanks, Lou. It'll be a date you won't forget," Dave said.

"That's what I'm afraid of."

As Lou approached the Union Avenue Mission, he saw Pete Johnson at the front desk. He'd been by the mission earlier in the investigation, and he knew Pete was a good guy. Lou rapped his knuckle on the glass. Pete looked up, smiled, and hurried to let him in.

"Hey, Pete, Lou Cros," he said as he opened his wallet to show his badge.

"Of course, Detective Cros. I remember you. What brings you back to the mission?"

"Just checking on things. Do you remember a man by the name of Pat Romans? He may have stayed here recently."

"Pat Romans? Can't say I do, but there're a lot of people who come and go. Can you tell me a little more about him? What does he look like?"

"Pretty average guy. About five-foot-six, one hundred twenty pounds, dark hair with some gray, probably in his early fifties."

"That describes most of the men we get. You think he stayed here?" Pete asked.

"Don't know. I do know he came by because he had one of your cards."

Pete's demeanor changed immediately.

"You're not telling me something. What is this about?"

"Another shooting victim was found this morning in the old Firestone tire building. He had one of your cards in his pocket."

"Dear God. I get a lot of people by here. I can't remember every one of them."

"What about your records? Do you show a Pat signing in or out in the last couple of weeks?" Lou pushed for an answer.

Pete opened the record book, which was on the front desk. A trickle of perspiration ran down the side of his cheek. Lou could tell he was nervous about the questioning. Flipping through the pages, Pete suddenly stopped. He looked startled. "Oh no! There was a Pat here last week. Yes, I do remember him. Came in for lunch and then left. Asked where Jim Damos was," Pete said.

"Was anyone with him? Or did you see anyone outside when he left?"

"Yes, yes, I did. A man who calls himself Joy Fully. He was with Pat."

"Do you see Joy often?"

"He has been coming by about every two weeks or so. He is a very caring person. He would never hurt anyone. Does Joy know about this? Oh, this is terrible. They won't blame anything on the mission, will they? There is so much good being done here."

"No, nobody is blaming the mission. Did you see anyone else hanging around Pat? Maybe some kids with punk hairdos?"

"No, I can't say I have," Pete replied. Pete took out his handkerchief and wiped his face.

"Who else helps at the mission? Do you have any help? Like a janitor or cook?"

"Yes, the man that helps out here is nicknamed Cotton. But he's been here since I started. Jim Damos brought him in to help out. He does a great job here."

"Is he here now?"

"No, we stagger our schedules."

"You know were he stays when he's not here?"

"He told me he stays at his son's house in Southaven."

"I'll need his real name and address."

"Sure, I can get that for you."

"What about when he's here? Does he have a room?"

"Yes, he has a room in the back."

"Mind if I take a look?"

"No, not at all."

Lou and Pete walked back to a small room that opened off the sleeping area. The room was a janitor's closet that had been equipped with a bed and a chest of drawers. It only took Lou a few minutes to search the area. Nothing of interest.

"If you remember anything else, give me a call. You still have my card?"

"Yes, it's by the phone. I'll call you if anything comes to mind. This is just terrible."

Lou left the mission and returned to the Beale Street area. It was still early, and he found himself walking south along the Main Street Trolley loop. Lou turned at the corner of Huling Avenue and walked to the Lorraine Motel on Mulberry Street, which was now the home of the National Civil Rights Museum. The historic landmark sign described the protest march by striking city sanitation workers that led to the assassination of Rev. Dr. Martin Luther King, Jr. on April 4, 1968.

Heading back toward Beale Street, Lou turned north on South Front Street and stopped at the Blue Monkey Bar and Grill for a cold beer. The bar was amazingly crowded for a Saturday afternoon. A bunch of loudmouthed kids with punk hairdos were sitting at a corner table. Five empty beer mugs were stacked on top of each other. The cheering started as the sixth mug was added. A male waiter sprang into action. Carrying four new mugs, he quickly disassembled the leaning glass tower. The kids at the table roared with laughter. Lou took a seat at the end of the bar within earshot of the group and ordered a glass of Bud Light draft.

"Those guys come here often?" he asked the bartender.

"Been in a couple of times. Drink for a few hours and leave. You a cop or something?"

"Nope, just here for a beer," Lou lied. "You got any peanuts?"

"Got a bag of chips."

"Pass."

"Hey, man!" yelled one of the guys. He had a Mohawk haircut and a beard. "We need some more beer. You got a pitcher?"

"Coming right up," the bartender said.

Lou downed his beer, threw a five-dollar bill on the bar, and started to leave.

"I told you I talked to Boots this morning. He was at home. Said he was in jail last night," boasted the bearded guy.

Lou sat back down and motioned for the bartender to bring him another beer.

"Shut up, Bones!" another kid shouted. "I told you to shut up!"

"Give me a break, J. Who cares?" Bones shouted back.

"I told you to shut up, Bones!" The kid named J. jumped up from his chair.

"All right, guys," the bartender said. "Finish what's in your mugs and get out, or I'll call the cops."

"Come on, let's get out of this crummy place," J. said.

J. was dressed in a pair of desert-colored camouflage pants, black combat boots laced to his shins, and a black T-shirt. His darker-than-normal jet-black hair was obviously dyed. It was cropped on the sides with long strings hanging down into his face. A black spiderweb tattoo bent around the left side of his neck. He appeared to be in his middle twenties, and he was close to six feet tall and had a muscular build. With no dog tags hanging around his neck, he looked more like a wannabe than an actual veteran.

Lou watched as the punks drank up and stacked their mugs on the table again. As they started to leave, J. kicked the table. The top two mugs fell from the tower, but nothing broke. Pushing through the front door, they all laughed and made some crude wisecracks about the bartender.

"Nice clientele you have here," said Lou.

"Bunch of weirdos. That'll be last time I let them in here."

Lou waited a minute to give the punks a head start, paid his bill, and wandered outside. Seeing them turn the corner, he followed them into the Beale Street District. The group disappeared into Silky O'Sullivan's. He checked his watch. It was almost six. He felt better knowing that Jack and Dave would be in the area that night.

When Lou arrived at Dyer's, Jack and Dave were already seated inside. Dave was munching on some onion rings. Two large iced teas sat on the table.

"I couldn't wait," said a grinning Dave. "I needed something to get me started."

Lou picked up a deep-fried onion ring and examined it.

"Is this grease from 2006 or 2007?"

"You tell me," joked Dave, pushing a plastic bowl of ketchup to Lou's side of the table.

Dipping his ring, Lou folded it into his mouth. "Definitely 2006," he said.

Once they placed their orders, Lou informed them about Randolph Booth, a.k.a. Boots, and the guy called J. They shared information about the Union Avenue Mission and the latest victim, and they talked about how all the pieces of the puzzle might fit together. A common thread seemed to be focused around Boots and J. Since both Jack and Dave were off duty and dressed in casual clothes, it would be a good time to split up and fall in with the crowds in the street. This way they could rotate, following J. and his group without anyone getting wise.

"Man, this is a lot of work for someone off duty," said Dave. "I'm going to need some more nourishment."

After finishing his onion rings, two deep-fried burgers, and a shake, Dave pushed back from the table and grinned. "Now, that's what I'm talking about," he said.

Jack relayed the story about the homeless man named Ted. "Pete Johnson at the mission said that Ted hasn't been by this week, but he has left a bag there. This is very unusual for a homeless person. Pete seems truly concerned about him. He's wondering where the guy is."

Dave and Lou nodded in agreement.

After leaving Dyer's, Dave crossed the street to check out the other eating establishments. His idea. Jack and Lou walked along together, and they stopped at the W. C. Handy Park for a beer and to listen to some music. It wasn't long before Lou heard J. and his group over the park music. From his vantage point, he saw them back on the street laughing and pushing each other around. Spots of spilled beer followed them like a shadow. As the night continued, the crowds and noise started to build. By ten o'clock, J. and his group had been thrown out of two bars and were content with sitting on the curb and insulting people as they walked by. It was a miracle that a fight hadn't started. Jack called the current officers on the beat. Within minutes, two officers stood in front of J. and his group. Walking them out of the Beale Street area, the party was over. Dave stopped by the park and handed Lou a bunch of two-for-one drink coupons that he had collected from the different restaurants.

"Thanks for dinner. Next time you can use the coupons. See you guys later. I'm out of here," said Dave.

As Lou and Jack left the park, a tall slender man stood on the corner with a Bible in his hand. His long sweat-drenched hair blended into his unshaven face. A couple of people sat on the grass and listened. Most just walked by as the preacher shouted, "In the last days, the love of the great body of people will grow cold! I feel the stains of death here tonight. Evil walks among us! I feel its presence. Darkness has come upon us all!"

The preacher paused. Lifting his arm, he pointed his crooked index finger at the crowd. It seemed to Lou that he was pointing directly at him.

"I know you, Satan! I know you by the fruit of your tree! Death is your fruit, and damnation is your soul."

Lou grabbed Jack's arm. "Let's get out of here. That guy is going to start a riot."

"I'm with you. He gives me the creeps. Where are you parked?" asked Jack.

"Riverside Drive."

"Yeah, me too."

Walking toward the river, Lou realized that he had to cross Front Street and the Cotton Row District. He felt a bit uneasy as they approached Front Street, and he was glad Jack was with him. A couple of kids jumped out from around the corner, laughed, and ran after each other.

"What the—!" yelled Lou. "Get out of here!" Grabbing one of them by his shirt, he flung him up against the building.

Jack grabbed Lou's hand. "It's okay. No harm done," said Jack, as he pulled Lou's hand loose.

"Yeah, no harm done," repeated Lou, letting go of the kid's shirt. "Sorry about that."

The kid pulled away, started running again, and yelled at Lou. "You idiot! Who do you think you are?"

"Lou, are you okay?" asked Jack. "You're shaking."

"Yeah, I'm fine. Let's get out of here," Lou said.

As Lou crossed Front Street, he saw a dark figure standing in the shadows along Cotton Row. First just one and then two. Within seconds, several more stood watching him as he walked by. Lou lowered his head and looked straight down as he crossed the street. His hands continued to tremble. His heart raced. His clothes were immediately covered with sweat.

"Jack, do you see anything down there?" Lou asked as he pointed down the street.

"No. Wait! I do see someone by the entrance of that building over there."

Jack stepped off the curb and turned in the silhouette's direction.

"Jack, don't go down there," Lou said. "It's nothing. Just a shadow. Just forget about it, okay?"

"No, I'm sure it's a person," insisted Jack.

At that moment, a man pushed away from the building and raced across the street. Just as he disappeared into an alley, a streetlight bounced off his face.

"That looked like Ted. The homeless guy I've been telling you about. You want to see if we can find him?"

"No, Jack! Let him alone!" yelled Lou.

"Okay, Lou. Calm down. Man, you're shaking."

"I'll be okay just as soon as I get away from here."

"Let's get you home. I'll call my buddies again and let them know what I saw. Maybe they can find Ted before something happens to him."

Lou hunched over and quickened his pace. Sweat dripped down the side of his face. Once he saw his car, he broke into a sprint.

"Slow down, Lou. You're going to have a heart attack," Jack shouted.

Lou jumped into his car. Unlocking his glove box, he took out his revolver and placed it on the seat next to him. Sitting behind the wheel, he tried to catch his breath.

Jack tapped on the window. "Lou, are you all right? You want me to drive you home?"

Lou took a deep breath and inched down the window. "I'm good, Jack. Just had a little anxiety attack. I'll be okay in a minute."

"I'm parked farther down. Call me on my cell if you need me. Okay?"

"Sure, Jack. Thanks."

Lou waited until Jack pulled out behind him. Waving in the rearview mirror, he signaled to Jack that he was fine. Feeling almost normal, he pulled out and headed up Union Avenue toward midtown. Just as he was crossing Main Street, a dark figure stepped out in front of his car and caused him to slam on the brakes. The tires squealed on the black asphalt. There was a slight thud as the man's body was thrown against the hood. Lou was frozen behind the wheel. The man's body slowly rose, until a towering figure stood erect in front of the car. His long hair dangled at his cheeks. Holding a book in both hands, he stretched out his long arms. Lou's hand touched his revolver.

"I know who you are! I know you by the fruit of your tree!" the preacher yelled.

Lou threw the car into reverse and slammed the gas pedal to the floor. The tires squealed again as the car pulled away from the man. Hitting the brakes, he crammed the gearshift back into drive, slammed the gas pedal to the floor again, and zigzagged around the standing figure. An oncoming car swerved and honked as Lou ran a red light.

How he got home, he didn't know. He felt angry and upset. He ran the visions over in his mind to try to find a reason for his sudden madness. The more he ran the images, the more upset he became. Throwing his keys on the kitchen table, Lou grabbed a bottle of Bacardi off the counter. Twisting off the cap, he took a long drink and sat down. His hands were still shaking. He took another drink and picked up an open bottle of aspirin off the table. Chewing three tablets, he washed them down with more rum. Feeling something heavy in his pocket, he took out his revolver and placed it on the table. Putting the bottle of clear liquid in front of the gun, he stared at the magnified misshapen barrel, which was seemingly distorted by the bottle. Noises on the street became amplified. Shadows on the wall started to close in on him. He felt a burst of cold air touch his cheek. He slowly reached around the bottle and placed his index finger on the trigger of the gun.

Chapter 4

The Shooter

Lou was jolted awake by the ringing of his cell phone. He fumbled through his pockets and found the culprit. Streams of light broke through the window blinds and bounced off the surrounding walls. Shadows hid in every recess of the room, as if waiting to attack a passerby. Rubbing his eyes, Lou straightened his aching back. Staring at the half-full bottle of rum, he wondered what he was doing at the kitchen table.

"Lou, you there?"

Lou recognized Jack's voice.

"I'm here. What time is it?"

"Ten thirty-five. You sound like I just woke you up."

"As a matter of fact, you did. What's up?" Lou asked.

"I got the name and address of the guy who was on Beale Street last night. The one called J. Name is Jason McKesson. Address is 1761 Stonewall. It's over in the midtown area, off Poplar Avenue. I had them run a rap sheet on the guy. No priors."

Lou looked around for something to write on. Finding nothing close, he wrote the information on the palm of his hand.

"Lou, is everything okay? You got a little crazy last night."

"I'm fine. Thanks for your help. You on duty today?" Lou asked, changing the subject.

"Not today. Got this Sunday off. I'm just going to relax and watch the Braves game. If you need anything, give me a call."

"Thanks, Jack."

After taking a cold shower, the pounding in Lou's head eased. Going back into the kitchen, he slid his revolver into his coat pocket. Seeing there was nothing in the refrigerator to eat, he headed to the Union Avenue Burger King. A cup of coffee would be a good start. Pulling into the parking lot, he spotted a familiar license plate. From outside, Lou saw Big John and Glitter. John was half sitting on a table, catty-corner from Glitter. Staring at the massive man, parents held their children close as they placed their orders. Somewhat tickled by the whole scenario, Lou ordered a cup of coffee and hurried over to the booth.

"Good morning, gentlemen. Am I interrupting your church service?"

"Church service," laughed Glitter, exposing his diamond tooth. "You're just too much. Sit a minute and drink your coffee. John was just leaving."

Glitter handed John some folded money and a note he wrote on a napkin. Lou assumed it was his next collection address. Glitter was dressed in his customary open-collar black shirt and sunglasses. Gold jewelry adorned his body.

"No need to leave, John. Stay for a minute, and I'll buy you a cup of coffee," Lou said.

Pushing Lou aside, John leisurely strolled out of the restaurant.

"Nice guy that John. Always full of conversation," Lou joked as he took a seat across from Glitter.

Glitter held up his gold-ringed fist and exchanged a knuckle tap with Lou. "Nice guy. Lou, you're a funny man," he laughed. "Now, don't you be harassing my comptroller. John is doing honest work, and I'm paying him well."

"I wouldn't think of harassing an honorable man. So are we all, all honorable men."

Glitter stared at Lou for a moment and then smiled. "I remember that quote. Somebody said that after Julius Caesar got knifed."

"I'm impressed," Lou said, grinning.

"And you thought I was just another pretty face," laughed Glitter. "Now, I know you didn't come here to drink coffee with me. What can I do you for?"

"I'm sure you heard about the murder at the old Firestone plant. Same MO as before. Did you hear anything about it on the streets?"

"You won't hear nothing if there wasn't drugs or money involved. You best start looking elsewhere. Streets are pretty upset with this whole thing. Don't feel safe for their kids. Something real strange about this."

"What can you tell me about a guy named Gary West? He works at the South Memphis Pawn on Third Street."

"Gary West? Can't seem to recall a Gary West," Glitter said.

Lou knew that Glitter was somehow involved in every pawnshop in south Memphis. Taking out a twenty-dollar bill, he dropped it on the table. "Maybe a cup of coffee will help your memory."

Glitter smiled as he picked up the bill. "I think maybe I do remember Mr. West. Believe he works nights. Big dude. Not much upstairs."

"Is he the kind of guy who might be selling stuff out the back door? Say, like a .38-caliber handgun?" Lou asked.

"Be pretty hard unless the owner is involved. Guns are checked every day. Firearm gnomes come by regularly and check the records. The only way it could go out the back door is if it never came in the front. West couldn't do it by himself. Too many security cameras. Besides, he ain't got the smarts."

"You know the owner?"

"He's an okay guy. Lives in a wheelchair. Served in Vietnam. Straight shooter. Like I said, you best be looking somewhere else."

"Thanks. Catch you later."

"Always a pleasure doing business with you. Drop in anytime."

"I'll do that."

Leaving the Burger King, Lou decided to check out Randolph Booth's place.

Parking his car a few blocks away, Lou walked toward the back of Boots's apartment. In the back of the two-story red brick building, sets of concrete stairs connected three breezeways. The second-floor balcony and black wrought-iron rail gave a hint that it could have been a renovated motel. There appeared to be six apartments per floor. Apartment 3C was on the top right. As Lou approached the parking lot, he saw Boots standing on the second-floor balcony, yelling at an elderly black man below. There was a black ragtop Jeep backed into a space near the stairs. Crouching down behind a parked van, Lou moved closer so that he could hear what they were saying.

"Hey, old man! You can't patch the parking lot without putting up some barriers! Cars will drive right over that crap!" yelled Boots.

The super looked up and pointed to a bunch of boxes in the grass.

"Yeah, well, that's great. They're doing a lot of good over there. You have to put them out as you go. What are you, stupid or something?"

The super smiled, waved, and continued with his work.

"Idiot!" yelled Boots.

Boots reentered the apartment. Within a few minutes, Boots and the guy Lou recognized as J. came out carrying boxes. It took them several trips to load the Jeep. Once it was loaded, they stopped by the apartment Dumpsters on their way out. Untying a trash bag, Boots turned it upside down and spread some shredded paper inside. Folding up the empty trash bag, he threw it into an adjacent Dumpster. As he returned to the Jeep, he saw the super watching him.

"Mind your own business, old man!"

The super turned away as the Jeep pulled out into the street. After the Jeep was out of sight, Lou approached the elderly black man, who was looking inside the Dumpster and talking to himself. As he got within earshot, the man turned and started complaining.

"Now, why would that kid do that? When they pick this up, that paper will blow all over everything. And I'm the one who will have to sweep up all the mess. What's wrong with kids today? They got no respect. Didn't get enough belt is their problem."

"Yes, sir. You're right. Kids today have it too easy," agreed Lou. "Please excuse me," he said as he showed the man his badge. "My name is Lou Cros. I'm an investigator for the Memphis Police Department. Do you work here?"

"Yes, I do. What can I do for you?"

"I'm looking into some issues with one of the tenants here. His name is Randolph Booth. He lives in apartment 3C. I believe he was the one yelling at you a minute ago."

A big grin came over the man's face. "Nothing would do me better than to see that rooster head out of here and behind bars. He's the one who dumped all these pieces of paper in the Dumpster. Then he and his Spiderman buddy tore out of here like they own the place. It'll make a real mess when the garbage truck comes. Real mean kid, he is. Got no respect. My name's J. C. Taylor. Just call me J. C. What can I do to help?"

"You called the other kid Spiderman. Do you know the other kid who was with him?"

"Yeah, I've seen him here before. I call him Spiderman. Has a spiderweb tattooed on his neck. What a pair those two are. Rooster head and Spiderman."

"You ever been inside Mr. Booth's apartment? I mean to fix something?" Lou continued.

"No, sir. He has made it real clear to the owners. He doesn't want anyone coming inside. He doesn't need to worry about that. He couldn't get me inside there. That man is evil."

Lou reached inside his pocket and pulled out a twenty-dollar bill. A grin came over his face. "You think I might be able to get a look inside?"

J. C. looked around the parking lot. Taking the money, he pointed to a box of tools on the grass. "Wouldn't be right not to help the police. There's a set of keys in the tray over there. Blue one is the master. If someone picked it up while I was working, I'd never know it."

"How long was the kid you call Spiderman here?" Lou asked.

"Not long. Loaded up a bunch of boxes. Seemed in a real hurry. I better get back to work. Nice talking with you. Stop by anytime." J. C. winked and walked away.

Lou unlocked the back kitchen door and entered quickly. Opening the refrigerator and ice section, he checked for anything unusual. All he found was a bunch of beer cans, half a loaf of bread, and some lunchmeats. Closing the door, he passed his hand behind the refrigerator and felt for any bags taped on the back. He quickly ran through the cabinets and drawers, but he found nothing of interest. As Lou entered the living room, he could tell that most of whatever was in it had been cleared out. Only a small TV, a sofa, and a coffee table were left, along with three card tables along the front wall. Pulling up the sofa cushions exposed a furniture rental tag. The card tables, TV, and stand all had the same tag. Moving through the rest of the apartment turned up no evidence. All the garbage cans were emptied, and nothing was under or inside the toilet tank. Taking a last look around, Lou checked the floor and air intake vents. All were clean. Whatever was there had been removed.

Leaving the apartment, Lou stopped by the toolbox tray in the parking lot and dropped the keys off, but something caught his eye. One of the boxes by the tool tray had a PDQ Delivery label on it. Examining the label, he saw where it was partially torn off. The only delivery letters left were R. Bo. The shipper label was also torn, which left only Pl Inc. LLC, Mex. Lou took the box across the parking lot to where J. C. was working.

"Excuse me, J. C. Where did you get these boxes?" asked Lou.

"From the Dumpster. I save the good ones. I can always use good boxes."

"Do you have any more with this PDQ label on them?"

"No, don't think so. Is it important?" asked J. C.

"Well, I don't know. It could be."

Lou quickly checked the other boxes, with no results. "If you see another one like this, give me a call," Lou said, handing J. C. one of his cards.

"Sure. I can do that."

"Oh, and, J. C., if you take your water hose and wet the paper down before the garbage truck comes by, it'll keep the paper from flying everywhere."

"Good idea. Thank you. I'll do that." J. C. smiled.

Passing by the Dumpster, Lou reached in and grabbed a handful of shredded paper. The diamond-cut shreds left behind little information. His first handful detailed more numbers than letters. Checking several times produced the same results. As Lou pulled out of the driveway where he had parked his car, he put a call through to Sue.

"Hi, what's up?" Sue asked.

"I'm heading over to Jason McKesson's house. He's one of Boots's buddies. The one they call J. The two of them cleaned out Boots's apartment this morning, so I have to assume they're taking the stuff over to McKesson's place. See what you can find out about him. I have his address as 1761 Stonewall Street in midtown. As far as I know, I don't think he has a clue that he's being watched. I just have a feeling that all this is related. Besides, I'm running out of leads. Anything on your end?" inquired Lou.

"No, not really. Where do we go from here?"

"I think we circle back and see if anyone remembers anything."

There was a short break in the conversation. Sue hesitated and then decided to speak up. "Are you doing okay?"

"Yes, why do you ask?"

"Well, don't get upset, but I understand you've been drinking more lately. Is there anything we need to talk about?"

"Yeah, you can tell Jack to mind his own business!" yelled Lou.

"Calm down, Lou. I'm only trying to help."

Realizing he was yelling, Lou took a deep breath and adjusted his volume.

"Sorry, I'm just dealing with my own demons. Kind of a Jekyll and Hyde syndrome. I'll be okay. I just need to clear my head a little more often."

"I think you're going about it the wrong way. Maybe you should give a call to the City Employee Assistance Program. It's all confidential."

Lou felt angry again. He needed to cut the conversation off.

"You've made your point! I'll discuss it with Mr. Hyde! I have to go."

"Call me later?" Sue asked.

"Will do," Lou replied.

Lou hung up his phone and threw it into the backseat. Grumbling to himself, he continued toward J.'s house.

Arriving on Stonewall Street, between Overton Park Avenue and Poplar, Lou looked at the old stone homes once owned by the affluent families of Memphis. Most were two- or three-story colonial-style houses with clay-tiled roofs. He remembered the court battle that began in 1969, when the state approved a nineteen-mile loop of I-40 through Overton Park and bought the right-of-way. A month after it all started, a conservation group filed a lawsuit in federal court to halt all construction. In 1971, Supreme Court Justice Thurgood Marshall mandated that the I-40 loop be shifted and that the Overton Park area be maintained. The decision came too late to save most of the homes. Overgrown lots separated the remaining homes that were bought up by investors for pennies on the dollar and turned into low-rent housing.

Circling the block, Lou passed the massive two-story stone home. A black Jeep was at the far end of the driveway. Parking in one of the empty lots, Lou approached the house from behind. Carefully watching the windows, he pressed himself against the chalk-white wood siding and inched toward the back porch. Through the screen, he was able to see several taped boxes. Not knowing if he would get this chance again, Lou made a decision to step inside and take a quick look in the boxes. Carefully pulling the tape back, he set the top of the box on the floor. Inside were dozens of computer components, a handful of plastic number pad sleeves with gas station logos, and a smaller business card-shaped box. The label read: Plastics, Inc. LLC, Mexico City, Mexico. Inside the card box were hundreds of blank magnetic strip debit cards. Just as Lou was retaping the box, he heard movement and a swishing sound behind him. Suddenly, he felt massive pressure on the back of his head. The force threw him forward onto the porch floor. Colors exploded though his vision. In a dazed state, voices were still audible.

"You hit that guy pretty hard, Boots. Who is he?"

"That's the cop I was telling you about!" Boots yelled, throwing a golf driver down on the floor.

"Boots, you clubbed a cop! What do we do now?"

"Shut up, J. Let me think a minute. Get some tape and let's cover his mouth and tape his hands and feet. He broke into your house, so he can't call us in, or he'll get busted. We can't call him in, or we'll get busted. Tape his hands in front so he can work his way loose. We don't need him dying on us. We need to get these boxes stored somewhere else. We'll get a storage building and hide them for now. Let's take this guy and dump him in one of the empty lots. The way I see it, he can't touch us without any evidence. We'll just have to watch our backs."

The voices faded. His mind filled with pictures as he lost consciousness.

In his vision, he saw the Firestone plant. There was a man sitting on the floor. An extended arm held a gun close to the man's head. Flickering candlelight danced the bizarre silhouette on the wall. Lou strained to gaze at the shooter's face. The ghastly face stared back through empty eye sockets. A blast of fire filled the room. Crimson blood seeped from a gunshot wound in the victim's head. The sitting man's body jerked backward against the wall and slowly fell to the floor. Everything went black.

"Mister! Mister! Are you okay?"

Lou felt a gentle shaking on his arm. The pain in the back of his head throbbed with every heartbeat. His clothes felt damp against his body. Slowly opening his eyes, Lou realized that his vision was blurred, but even so, he could see two kids looking at him. From what he could tell, they appeared to be around ten years old. One was standing back, supporting two bikes. From the low light in the background, Lou could tell it was around dusk. Overgrown sun-bleached grass surrounded him.

"Mister, are you a gangster?" asked the boy closest to him.

Reaching up with his taped hands, Lou peeled the tape off his mouth.

"No, I'm a cop," he replied.

"I think he's a gangster," stated the other boy.

"I'm not a gangster. I'm a cop. Can you help me with this tape?" Lou extended his hands toward the boys.

"Don't do it," said the other boy. "We need to call the cops."

"I *am* a cop," Lou insisted. "Look in my coat pocket. I have a badge and ID."

The boys stared at each other for a minute. "What do you think?" one asked the other.

"Okay, but if you move, we'll call the cops."

"I am a cop," Lou repeated, trying to stay calm.

The boy carefully reached into Lou's pocket and pulled out his badge wallet. Opening it up, he showed it to the other boy.

"What's your name?" asked the kid, checking the ID.

"Lou Cros."

"What's your badge number?" he asked, smiling at the other boy.

Lou's head was pounding, and he hesitated a minute to clear his mind. "286, 789."

"Where do you live?"

"That's enough! Either you take this tape off me, or I'm going to run you in for obstruction of justice!"

"Okay, man. Chill out." Finding the end of the tape, one of the boys unwrapped Lou's hands and backed away.

Freeing his ankles, Lou felt the back of his head. There was some crusted blood in his hair, but not much. Trying to get up, he lost his balance and fell back down to a sitting position.

"Where am I?" Lou asked.

"You're over by Overton Park Zoo," stated the boy closest to him. "We cut through this field when we're late. Did some gangsters try to kill you and dump you here?"

Seeing he wasn't going to get away from this questioning, Lou conceded, "Yes, a couple of gangsters kidnapped me and dumped me here. You boys are heroes."

"I knew it," smiled the boy holding the bikes. "Will we get a medal or something?"

"Well, you'll get something." Reaching into his pants pocket, Lou pulled out two ten-dollar bills. "Here, for noteworthy assistance in apprehending gangsters. Now, may I have my badge and ID back?"

Satisfied with their reward and the best summer story ever, the boys jumped on their bikes and sped off. Lou sat for a minute and rubbed his temples. He couldn't remember anything from the time he was hit until now. Lou figured that he could make an anonymous call and tip off the Feds about the debit card fraud. That way, he could be sure Boots and his friends got busted. He knew that the equipment he saw was a skimming device. These devices were plastic sleeves that could be glued over a keypad. They were molded and painted to match that on an ATM or gas pump, making them hard to detect. Their design was to capture credit or debit card numbers and pin codes.

Finding his way back to his car, Lou drove past by J.'s house on the way out. All the lights were off, and the Jeep was gone. He felt sure that they had already moved the boxes to another location. He would let the Feds deal with them.

Driving by Overton Park, Lou decided to pull over and let his mind clear. He pulled into the overgrown parking lot of an old outdoor theater named the Overton Park Shell, which was closed in 2004. He remembered that Elvis had done his first paid performance there in 1954. He also recalled that his last visit to the Shell was in 2003, when Ricky Nelson was inducted into the Rockabilly Hall of Fame, and Ricky's sons, Gunnar and Matthew, gave a live performance. Lou walked down to the bench seating. Some construction materials were laid along the concrete pad in front of the stage. Renovations had been started over a year before to bring the outdoor theater back to its days of glamour, but tight city budgets had slowed the pace.

Bypassing a construction barrier, Lou sat on the back row of benches. He recalled when Sue first started with the police department. He had run into her at this very place. She was jogging through the park and stopped to listen to a Saturday afternoon concert. Lou tried to remember why he was there but wasn't able to pull the information from the recesses of his rattled brain. She had her hair pulled back in a ponytail and tied with a blue ribbon. She wore a dark blue jogging outfit and white Nike tennis shoes. They talked about the police department and how much she was looking forward to becoming a detective. Her smile was radiant and her laughter intoxicating. Lou was smitten from the first day.

Rubbing the knot on his head, Lou put his wandering mind back on the case. There had to be a link. All three victims were homeless people. Of the three victims, he knew two had contact with the Union Avenue Mission. He had to assume that the third victim probably did too. That put Pete Johnson, Jim Damos, and the man called Cotton in touch with the victims. Lou had known Jim too long to think he was the killer, and so he put him aside. Pete Johnson seemed to be at the right place to have committed the murders, but at the wrong time. He didn't fit. Cotton was still on his list. Lou considered Boots and J. as small-time punks out to make a dollar. He would put them aside for now and let the Feds work them over.

Glitter had made a good point. There was no apparent financial motive behind the killings. There didn't seem to be sexual motive. So, the serial killer was most likely driven by emotion. As Glitter said, "It could be one of their own." That left just one suspect at the top of the list. Lou knew what he had to do. He had to find this man. A man named Ted.

CHAPTER 5

Ted

JACK TOOK A HARD look around the Beale Street District. Mondays were usually slow. The weekend sports enthusiasts and party animals had already left for home. Street and sidewalk scrubbers inhaled the weekend trash and left behind a damp trail of excrement. Intern barkers paced the doorways to impress the restaurant owners, who took little notice of their show. Music blared through open doors as it competed for air space. Kids raced around, giving away two-for-one coupons to anyone who would take the bait.

Jack had received a call from Captain Smitters earlier in the day. It was a strange call, to say the least, but personal enough that it got Jack's full attention. The request to double the patrols in the district must have come from the mayor. The editorial page in yesterday's *Commercial Appeal* had given the killer a typically hyperbolic name, calling him or her the Memphis Mangler. As a result of the editorial, the mayor's office had been flooded with calls.

Commercial Appeal. Sunday, June 10, 2007

It seems that City Hall has once again tried to cover up information. This time, they have put our lives in danger for the receipts of Memphis in May Festival. It seems that a serial killer is on the

Memphis streets. The Memphis Mangler struck for a second time during the last week of the festival on Riverside Drive at Tom Lee Park. This reporter has just recently found out that a third murder has taken place at the old Firestone plant on Firestone Avenue. All three victims were homeless people, who seem to be of no concern to City Hall. The only comment this reporter could get from the mayor's office was "No comment."

"Did you ever reach Lou?" asked Dave.

"I called him several times on Sunday afternoon after I read the newspaper. No luck," replied Jack. "I must have left three or four messages on his cell phone. The captain is pretty hot that he couldn't be reached. I'm sure by now Captain Smitters has given him an earful."

"I'm getting sort of hungry. How about you?" Dave asked.

"Okay, I'd hate to see you waste away. Let's make a stop by the mission and see if anyone has seen Ted. Then we can take a walk down Beale Street."

Dave waited in the patrol car as Jack pushed the door buzzer. Pete Johnson peeked out from the back and waved his hand to acknowledge Jack's presence. The door lock buzzed open. Entering the mission, Jack found Pete sitting in an office eating a Subway sandwich.

"Welcome, good to see you again. Just finishing up my dinner," stated Pete, wiping his mouth with a napkin. "What brings you out tonight?"

"Just wanted to see if you heard from Ted. Did he show up?"

"I meant to call you about him. Time just got away. He stopped in about two hours ago. He was real upset. Had a bad cut on his cheek. I made him sit down, and I cleaned it up. I asked him a couple of times if anyone hurt him. He kept saying, 'Nobody. Nobody hurt me.' The whole thing was real odd."

"What do you think he meant by that?"

"I don't know. He kept getting up and looking out the door like he was expecting someone. I asked him who he was looking for, and he said he was being followed. Said it wasn't safe here at the mission anymore."

"Did he say where he was staying?"

"I asked him where he was staying, and he said with friends. Friends who protect him. Didn't make a lot of sense, but he was very nervous about being here. He grabbed his things from the back and kept watching the street. I made him a little to-go bag and asked him if he knew who was following him. He said he didn't. I asked him again if anyone hurt him. He said, 'Nobody.' It was like that guy who told that Cyclops monster that his name was no man, and then blinded him. The monster kept saying that no man had hurt him. You know what I'm talking about?"

"I think you're referring to Homer's *Odyssey*."

"That's the one. I tried to get him to stay, but he said he had to get to his friends to protect him. He seemed really scared."

"Which way did he go when he left?"

"Straight up Union Avenue toward the river."

Dave beeped in on Jack's radio. "We got a disturbance call at Silky O'Sullivan's. Guy with a knife threatening someone."

"Ten-four, Dave. Be right out," Jack said. He nodded in Pete's direction and said, "Thanks. Call me if Ted shows up again." Jack headed out the door.

"Yes, of course," Pete said to Jack's back.

Jumping into the patrol car, Jack headed over to the Beale Street District. Silky O'Sullivan's was on the east end of Beale and only a couple of minutes away.

"What do you have?" asked Jack.

"Seems some big guy came in and approached two customers at a table. One of the guys at the table starts yelling and pulls a knife. Nobody's hurt yet."

"Must be a full moon," Jack said.

Rushing into Silky's bar, Jack and Dave saw that Big John Fagan had two guys pinned in a corner behind a circular table. One of them was cursing and waving a knife from side to side. John pushed the massive wooden table as if it was on wheels and cut the two at the waist. Leaning over the table, John estimated the closed position of the swinging knife and delivered a crushing blow to the man's jaw. The sound of breaking bone was unmistakable as the man dropped the knife and bounced off the wall. He slumped over the table, out cold from the knockout blow. The other man stared in disbelief and quickly held his hands up, as if John had a gun on him. Jack took his hand off his gun, knowing he probably wouldn't need it. He had dealt with Big John a couple of times in the past and was familiar with his background.

"We'll take it from here, John. Please back away from the table," Jack said.

Big John took a step back, holding his stare at the other man. Placing his foot over the knife, he slid it back toward Jack and Dave.

"Anyone here see what happened?" asked Jack, moving in to check on the man slumped over the table. "Anybody?"

"Yeah, I saw it," replied a waiter behind the bar. "The big guy walked in and started talking to the two guys at the table. The guy behind the table got real loud and pulled out a knife. That's when I called the cops."

"You got anything to add?" Jack asked the other man.

Looking over at John, the man swallowed hard. "No, sir. That's what happened. I didn't have anything to do with this. I didn't know he had a knife. He just had too much to drink, that's all."

"Dave, take down these guys' names and addresses. That one can go when you're through," said Jack as he pointed to the man standing behind the table. "This one will need an ambulance. Looks like his jaw may be broken." Turning to the waiter, Jack continued, "We'll need to get a statement from you. Doesn't look like anything is damaged. You want to press charges?"

"No, I called my boss. He said just get them out of here."

"John, do you want to press any assault charges?"

Big John looked over at Jack but made no response.

"I'll take that as a no. You're free to go, but don't leave town in case we need to get back to you. I believe we still have your current address."

Big John slowly backed away and headed toward the door. As he walked outside, the bar crowd separated like the Red Sea. He lit a cigarette and stood around to see what was going to happen. Within minutes, an emergency crew showed up. After wrapping the man's chin, the EMTs placed him on a stretcher and loaded him into the ambulance. Leaving the bar, Jack and Dave dispersed the crowd. Big John crossed the street and headed toward his car. Crowds of people fell in behind him. Halfway down the street, he noticed that a man with a muscular build was watching him. The man was six feet tall and in his early forties. He was wearing a black T-shirt and blue jeans. His black wavy hair and goatee were neatly trimmed. A pair of snakeskin cowboy boots finished off his attire. As John passed him, the man fell in behind the crowds.

Big John cut through an alleyway and left the Beale Street District. Stopping at the next corner, he lit another cigarette. Turning his head a little to the side, he glanced back. A block away, he saw a figure dart into an alcove. Big John took a few drags off his cigarette and started walking back toward Beale Street. When he got within fifty feet of where he had seen the figure, he leaned against a storefront and waited. In a few seconds, part of a head peeked out and immediately sprang back. Taking another drag off his cigarette, Big John flicked it out into the street. The red flame split and bounced on the asphalt. Closely watching for another movement, he directed his question to the dark alcove.

"Feeling lucky?" he asked.

A young couple turned the corner on the other side of the street. Laughing loudly, the man stumbled and spilled part of his beer. Laughing it off, he turned up the plastic cup and finished off the remaining suds. The girl started to run, holding her beer out at arm's length.

"You're not getting mine!" she teased.

The young man threw his empty cup into the street and took off after his girlfriend.

Distracted for only a few seconds, Big John spotted the man in black darting back around the corner. Lighting another cigarette, he turned and walked away, not giving the suspicious man much more thought.

By now it was almost seven, and Dave was complaining about his sides caving in from hunger. Deciding on some Cajun cuisine, Jack and Dave stopped at the outside counter of the Rum Boogie Café. Dave ordered a cup of gumbo, and he polished it off with a bowl of red beans and rice. Jack picked at his jambalaya and ended up throwing most of it away. As Jack relayed the story of Ted to Dave, the two walked toward the Cotton Row District. The sun was low in the western sky, casting shadows along Front Street. This was the last place Jack thought he had seen Ted. Jack knew each building had multiple floors with dozens of offices. If Ted were hiding in one of the old cotton-sample warehouses, he would be almost impossible to find. Jack figured it would take them over an hour just to check one building for forced entry. The situation was magnified by the fact that every building had been closed for decades, and every window and door was a point of entry.

Jack noticed a broken padlock hasp on an alley door of one of the cotton office buildings. He pushed his way in. Dirt-coated windows along the alley side gave just enough light to expose the entryway. A dusty wooden floor was centered between a set of stairs and an old brass gate that stood as an elevator door guard. Crumbling newspapers and boxes were braced against the cracking plaster walls. Electrical wires poked out from the ceiling where elaborate brass lighting once hung. A cracked glass frame attached to the north wall announced the offices of the cotton merchants. The dark-wood office doors were seven feet tall, each with a frosted glass panel that reflected the tenant's hand-painted name.

Checking several offices on the first and second floors, Jack and Dave climbed the last flight of stairs to the third floor. The office door to the left of the stairs read M. Aura & Company, Cotton Office. The door was ajar, and when Jack pushed it open, the dim sunlight from the warehouse windows showed through. Two dusty desks stood in the front office, along with two bulging trash cans. Brown paper wrappings cluttered the floor. A framed print of a U.S. Navy battleship rested on the top of the back desk. Wiping the dust off the bottom of the frame, Jack was able to read the name: USS *Tennessee*, 1920–1959.

"Look at this," said Jack as he waved Dave over. "My dad was in the navy. We had a similar print at home when I was growing up. The USS *Tennessee* was one of eight battleships present at the attack of Pearl Harbor. Two bombs hit the ship, but it didn't sink. It came back from the shipyard after repairs in the early forties and supported the Iwo Jima operations. It was decommissioned in 1947, and then it became part of the Atlantic Reserve Fleet until 1959. This print is a treasure." Seeing a hook in the wall, Jack wiped the dust off the glass and hung the print over the desk.

"Well, why not take it with you? Nobody here will care," joked Dave.

"No way. The ghosts of Cotton Row will care," teased Jack. "I'm not going to disturb their house."

"Funny. You're a funny man. I don't believe in ghosts. Don't tell me you believe in all that mumbo jumbo?"

"I guess you're going to tell me you've never heard of the National Register of Haunted Places?"

"Man, don't feed me that stuff," Dave said. "It's all a crock."

"Really? Well, you'll be glad to know that Memphis has a Paranormal Investigations Team. It has identified more than fifteen haunted places right here in Memphis. The Orpheum Theatre is one, along with the Libertyland Theme Park, Audubon Park, Chase Mansion, and Voodoo Village."

"Man, you're making this up," Dave said.

"I'm not. You need to take the Memphis Ghost Tour through the downtown alleys. Check it out for yourself. Google it. It's all there."

Dave moved into the inner office. "Here's a funny print. Look at this one," he called to Jack. When Jack came in, Dave held up a framed print of what looked like a hobo, who was wearing a red coat, a brown hat, and a black shoelace bowtie. He was sitting in a rocking chair on top of the earth. At the bottom of the print was a title: "The Gay Philosopher Sitting on Top of the World." The print was signed by Henry Major.

"And I guess you're not going to take it, either?" Dave asked.

"Nope. It belongs here with its owners."

Walking through the inner office, Jack stepped into the sample room.

Three rows of empty tables stretched from one end to the other. Specks of rusty-colored cotton fibers peeked out from tiny splinters of the black-painted wood. Florescent light fixtures appeared to be suspended in midair as they hung from the metal ceiling, which was painted white. A red Coke machine stood in front of the windows that lined the alley. Its door was open, exposing the mold-spotted white plastic interior and metal shelves. Next to the machine, propped against a folded card table, was a handmade checkerboard. A small stack of dust-free brown corrugated boxes was neatly arranged in the far corner, indicating they had been used recently.

"Somebody's been here," stated Jack. "Probably sleeping on these boxes. Look here. Some melted candle wax. It looks like whoever it was has moved on. They don't like to stay in one place for long."

Dave nodded his head in agreement. "Starting to get dark in here. We better find our way out before the ghosts wake up," Dave said, chuckling.

"Yeah, you're right. We need to get back to Beale Street," said Jack, trying to sound as serious as he could. "They usually come out when the sun goes down." Dave's smile immediately disappeared. "Let's get out of here," pressed Jack, holding back his grin.

On the third floor of another empty building, Ted struck a match and lit a small white candle. The candlelight danced around the third-floor cotton-sample room. Old black-and-white photos of past cotton merchants leaned against the surrounding walls.

"You never told me your name," whispered Ted.

Two eyes flickered back at him. No response.

Opening his mission bag, Ted took out a small bottle of water. "We're safe here. Our friends will protect us," he said, motioning toward the photos that lined the wall. "I saw that man today. The one who's following me. He didn't see me, but I saw him. Did you see him?"

The eyes showed no response.

"Guess not." Looking inside the mission bag, Ted continued. "I told Mr. Johnson about you." He touched the bandage on his cheek. "I hope you don't mind. I called you Mr. Nobody, since I don't know your name. Can't you tell me your name?"

The nonblinking eyes delivered no response.

"I like Mr. Johnson. He doesn't pressure me. Do you know him? You would like him. I don't think I can go there anymore. That man will find me. You can stay with me. We're safe here. We're with friends. Don't worry. I'm going to Jackson, Mississippi, when it's safe. I have friends there too. Do you want to go with me?"

Mr. Nobody took a step closer. He held his stare. The movement went unnoticed.

Taking a pack of peanut butter crackers from his bag, Ted opened the packet and held it close to his nose. "Peanut butter. I love the smell of peanut butter. It reminds me of when I lived in St. Louis. Dad always brought home peanut butter and bananas from the store. He liked that." Ted shivered for a moment as the picture of his dad's suicide flashed through his mind. Stretching out his arm, he offered a cracker to Mr. Nobody. The cat backed away.

"I'm not going to pick you up. I know you don't like that," Ted said, touching the bandage on his cheek again. Ted stared at the candlelight. His surroundings began to spin. Dropping the cracker, a familiar metal taste entered his mouth. Random twitching started in his upper body and consumed him in seconds. Mr. Nobody expelled a sinister hiss and quickly escaped through an open door. As if pulled by the strings of a puppeteer, Ted collapsed on the floor. Spittle dripped from the corner of his mouth, and his eyes rolled backward into his head. Strange images flashed through his jumbled mind, interspersed with splashes of black and red.

A man's head lay sideways in a puddle of blood. His face morphed between a homeless friend and his father. Sounds of footsteps magnified as they crushed pieces of newspaper. Running in slow motion, he found the abandoned mechanical room and climbed the ladder to the gravel roof. Peering over the parapet wall of the Firestone building, he saw someone in the shadows of the apartments across the street. The figure looked up. Eye contact was made. Fear shot through his body, almost immobilizing him, but then he ran to the back of the roof, climbed down a broken roof ladder, and fell fifteen feet to the ground. Running along the railroad tracks, he stopped next to a wooden electrical pole and looked back. In the darkness, a flash of light ignited. A bullet tore a thumbnail hole into the wood pole. A piece of splintered wood stung his face.

The seizure lasted only a few seconds. When Ted regained consciousness, his body ached, and his clothes were soaked with sweat. A small mouse scurried away from the peanut butter cracker that lay on the floor next to a puddle of melted wax. Taking deep breaths, Ted struggled with the stale air. Wiping the spittle from the corner of his mouth, he took a drink of water to help remove the dry, metallic taste.

As if by magic, Mr. Nobody descended from the top of a sample table onto the scurrying prey below. A horrid squeal echoed off the warehouse walls. Needing some fresh air, Ted wobbled to his feet as the spinning room came to a stop. Feeling his way along the dark stairwell, he exited out the side alley emergency door. Taking a piece of broken Popsicle stick out of his pocket, he forced it into the mechanism, disabling the autolock.

A fine mist of rain soothed his sun-leathered skin. Walking close to the Cotton Row buildings, he continued down the street to Confederate Park. Leaning on the stone wall, Ted looked at the lights of the Hernando DeSoto Bridge reflecting off the black Mississippi River in the distance. Realizing that the wall exposed him, he stepped back and accepted the safety of one of the park's giant oaks. A gust of wind seemed to shout a warning at him, as if the leaves rustling against each other were a multitude of strange voices that called to him, urging him to be careful, screaming together that there was danger.

"I hear you, my friends," he whispered, bracing himself against the massive trunk. At the other end of the park, a tree trunk's outline moved and disappeared into the darkness. The shifting wind briefly parted the leaves and opened up spots of light from the street. A metal object blinked. Crouching down, Ted quickly approached the stone wall and climbed over it. Working his way down the steep levee, he hit the bottom of the hill and turned back toward the safety of Cotton Row. A flash appeared at the top of the hill. A bullet spit a spray of dirt five feet from him. Continuing down Riverside Drive, Ted cut through the first street and entered into the alleys of Cotton Row.

Pressing himself against one of the buildings, he watched the alley entrance. A dark figure appeared and seemed to stare down the alley. The back lighting behind the figure made it impossible for Ted to make out any features of his hunter. He held his breath, afraid of making any noise that might reveal his presence. In a few seconds, the figure moved away.

Chapter 6

Premonition

Big John Fagan stirred in his bed. Something had disturbed his sleep. The Vollentine Court Apartments were far from safe. John had lived in the low-rent housing in north Memphis for nearly a decade. After the closing of the nearby Dixie-Mart Carondelet department store and the development of a housing project around the corner on North Watkins, drugs, alcohol, violence, and prostitution became common.

Big John wiped the sweat from his face. The small box fan and window unit were silent. It wasn't unusual for the power to go off, but something was different. He heard music playing in the apartment above his. Sitting up in bed, Big John reached for a bottle of beer that was left over from the night before. Taking the last few sips, he returned the bottle to the nightstand. From the sound of the traffic and the apartment noise, he figured it was around 3:00 or 4:00 AM. Picking up a partially smoked cigarette from the ashtray, he found his lighter and lit up. He heard a small movement in the hallway, like someone had brushed up against the wall. Big John quickly put down the cigarette, freeing both hands. Reaching down along the bed, he removed a Colt Agent .38-caliber Special that was holstered to the bed frame. Standing next to the bedroom doorway, with his back to the wall, he waited. A dark figure stepped through the open bedroom door. Big John grabbed the intruder by the neck and slammed him against the door. Three rounds echoed in the apartment. The music in the apartment above was turned up.

Sitting in the old parking lot on Riverside Drive, Lou stared at the side of an abandoned building. Years ago, the building was used by General Electric to manufacture small auto lightbulbs. Several decades had passed since the auto bulb manufacturing had moved overseas for low-cost labor. The deteriorating building told the story of the lost jobs.

"Gum?" Sue offered Lou a stick of Big Red.

"Yeah, thanks."

"So, Captain Smitters came down on you pretty hard?"

"He made me feel like a rookie," replied Lou.

"Lou, you said you couldn't find your cell phone and had lost track of the time. You had several cell phone calls, and you didn't answer any of them or even check in with the office. Then you tell me you found your phone in the backseat of your car. Sounds like a rookie move to me."

"Okay, enough already!" Lou rubbed the knot on the back of his head. "Smitters threatened to pull me off the case if anything like this happens again." Frustrated, Lou added another thought. "We still need to backtrack. Somebody must have seen something. I'd like you to follow up on a man at the mission. Fellow works there they call Cotton. See what you can find out about him."

"Okay, what else?"

"Smitters told me that the Feds picked up Boots and his buddy J. They found some used debit card-skimming equipment at J.'s house, and he spilled his guts about Boots. I don't think we need to worry about them anymore."

They sat in silence for the next few minutes.

"What brought you here?" Sue asked.

"I'll never forget this place." Lou looked out at the aging building. Jagged pieces of broken glass filled the oxidized metal window frames. Flakes of blue paint, blistered by the sun, lay at the feet of the concrete block wall. Weeds had sprouted up through the cracking asphalt as nature slowly reclaimed the area. A pigeon flew out one of the broken windows, landed, and strutted along the foundation, as if it was a sentry guarding against any intruder.

"Lou, you need to forget it and move on with your life."

"I'll never forget."

A few more minutes of silence passed.

"Have you noticed the man across the street?" asked Sue. "I think he's watching us. He could have filled up four or five cars by now."

Lou looked in his rearview mirror. A man was pumping gas at a market across the street. He lingered at the pump after it had finished.

"Let's do a drive-by," Lou said.

As Lou's car pulled out of the parking lot, the man put the fuel nozzle back in the pump. Passing by an adjacent pump, Lou tried to get a look at the guy. The man ducked his head to hide his face and got back into his car. The only thing Lou could catch was a quick view of his snakeskin boots. The man left before he could get into position to stop his advance.

"Did you get his license number?" asked Lou.

"Got it. I'll check it out and see who our mystery guest is."

Dropping Sue off at her car, Lou turned onto Poplar Avenue and headed to the Tennessee Mental Health Center to see Joy Fully. Filling out the visitation information forms, Lou was led to Dr. Walter Sims's office. Entering the office, he handed over the paperwork.

"Please take a seat," the doctor said, motioning him to sit down. Pressing a button on the side of his desk, an orderly entered the office and stood with his back against the door.

"You got some pretty tight security here, Doc."

"It's necessary for the patients' safety." The doctor spoke softly while reading over the forms. Once he had finished, he placed the forms in a folder on his desk.

"This all looks in order, Detective Cros. You will be allowed to visit Mr. Philaski in a moment, but first I want you to know that he is being medicated. If he shows any stress or agitation during your visit, you will be asked to leave. Do you understand?"

"Yeah, sure, Doc."

"Do you have any questions for me at this time?"

"Have you located any of his family?"

"Yes, we have located his brother in Cleveland, Ohio. Mr. Joel Philaski—you know him as Joy Fully, I suspect—was born in Cleveland. His brother is due here this afternoon. Personal and medical information on Mr. Philaski will have to be withheld pending his brother's written consent. I'm sure you understand."

"Sure. You mentioned he is on medication. Will it affect his memory?"

"We have noticed a little decrease in his cognitive responses, and his long-term memory seems flawed."

"Is that a yes or a no?" asked Lou, showing a slight smile for the first time.

"That's a maybe, Detective Cros," replied the doctor, holding a straight face.

"I will need his brother's information for the investigation."

"That information has already been sent to—" The doctor interrupted himself, pausing as he opened a file folder on his desk. "We sent it on to a Captain Smitters. Will you need anything else?"

"No, that's all, Doc."

"Very well. Mr. Lance will be taking you to the ward," the doctor said as he motioned toward the orderly standing at the door. "When you are through, he will assist you with the security elevator. There is no need for you to check out. Mr. Lance will handle that for you."

"Okay, Lurch, let's go," joked Lou, trying to get a smile out of the placid faces.

"Lance, sir. My name is Bill Lance."

"Lighten up, Lance. You guys are way too serious around here."

"Yes, sir." Bill forced a smile as they left the office and walked down the hallway.

"How long have you worked here?" Lou asked.

"This is my second year at this facility."

"Yeah? Where you from?"

"St. Louis."

Lou's investigative juices began to flow. Bill Lance was close to six feet three inches tall, with short cropped salt-and-pepper hair. Lou guessed his age to be around forty-five. His portly build carried two hundred fifty to two hundred seventy pounds. He wore an elevated sole and heel on his left shoe that helped cover up his uneven gait and slight limp. A small tattoo of a parachute barely showed through the heavy hairs on the back of his forearm.

"I love St. Louis. What a great city. You go to school up there?" Lou asked.

"Yes, sir. St. Louis University."

"No, kidding! I have a good friend who graduated from there. What year did you graduate?"

"Nineteen eighty-five," Bill replied.

"I noticed the parachute on your arm. I appreciate your service. Army?"

"Yes, sir. Served in Desert Storm. Early discharge." Bill tapped his left leg. "Shattered my leg in a jump."

"So, how do you like working here?"

"It's a good job. Hours are flexible. Good benefits." He stopped at a double door. "Here we are, Detective Cros. The attendant will page me when you're ready to go."

"Thanks, Lance. I'll see you in a bit."

Opening the double door, the attendant made a note of the time on his clipboard and showed him to the ward. Joy Fully was standing in front of a barred window.

"Hi, Joel," Lou said, using Joy's real name instead of his street name. He was curious to see if the man responded to it. "It's Lou Cros. Do you remember me?" Lou said to Joy's back.

No reaction.

Okay, let's try this again, Lou thought. "Joy, it's Lou Cros. We met at the old Firestone plant the night you found your friend Pat. Do you remember me?"

Joy turned away from the window and said, "Why, yes, of course, Mr. Cros. I remember you. Are you here to take me home?"

"No, Joy, I'm afraid not. I'm here to ask you a few questions about the day you were at the Firestone plant. Do you remember that day?"

"Yes, I remember. An officer took my flashlight. You gave me another one. I'm sorry, Mr. Cros, but I've misplaced it. Did you want it back?"

"No, Joy. It's yours."

"Thank you, Mr. Cros." Joy turned away and stared out the window again.

Lou noticed that Joy didn't move his fingers like he had before when they spoke at the crime scene.

"I don't like this place, Mr. Cros. It makes me sad," he said with his back to Lou. His voice was barely above a whisper. Then he faced Lou again, and Lou noticed that he really did look sad.

"It's very strange," Joy said. "When you are outside, people treat you like you are invisible. When you are inside, people lose trust in you. I don't know where I belong. Can you see me, Mr. Cros?"

"Yes, Joy, I can see you."

"Sometimes, people don't see me. It makes me sad."

"Sad like the day you found your friend Pat?" asked Lou.

"Yes, sad like that."

Lou took his first look around the ward. An attendant stood inside the room, his back to the wall. Several people in robe-covered pajamas sat in front of a wall-mounted TV. An elderly woman was playing solitaire on a card table. A young man sat in a chair, turning the pages of a book so quickly he couldn't possibly be reading. Everyone was quiet.

"You told me that when you went inside and found Pat, he was laying on the floor. Is that right?"

"Yes, he was just lying there. It made me sad."

"Do you remember hearing anything or seeing anyone before you entered the building?" asked Lou.

"No, I didn't see anyone."

"What about any cars? Did you see any cars? Do you remember any lights on the street?"

"No, Mr. Cros. I'm sorry."

"When you went outside to find the police, what about then?"

Joy turned away and stared out the window again. A couple of minutes went by. Lou let him think.

Several more minutes passed in silence.

"Joy?" Lou asked, his voice gentle.

No response.

Joy's fingers began twitching as he slowly turned around, facing Lou again.

"Joy, it's Lou Cros."

"Yes, Mr. Cros. Did you come to take me home?"

"No, Joy. We were talking about when you went outside to find the police. The night you found Pat. Did you see anyone outside the building?"

"No, I didn't see anyone," Joy replied.

"Thank you, Joy. You've been a big help."

"You are welcome, Mr. Cros." Turning away, Joy stared out the window again. "This place makes me sad," he said.

It made Lou feel sad too.

Lou left the ward. He let Bill Lance know he was done with the interview, and then he left the hospital. He decided to cut over to Union Avenue. His cell phone rang.

"Lou, it's Jack Mills."

"What's up?"

"I'm at Big John Fagan's apartment. There's been a shooting. Big John is dead."

"Do you know what happened?"

"Apparently the guy he brushed with at Silky's bar came by for a little

82

revenge. Big John took three slugs in his chest, but he still managed to reach his shooter. Crushed his windpipe. Shooter's dead too. Feds are here. Smitters is hot. Any idea why the Feds were called in?"

"No, not just yet, but I'll get back with you. What kind of hardware was the shooter packing?"

"Old .32 caliber, with the serial number filed off, of course. Big John had a Colt Agent with no rounds fired."

"Thanks for the call, Jack. If I find anything out, I'll give you a call."

Lou hit End and closed the cell. He headed straight to the Union Avenue Burger King in hope of finding Glitter. Just as he pulled into the parking lot, Glitter was leaving the building. A flash of gold blinked from around his neck.

"Hey, Lou," said a grinning Glitter. "Thought I might be seeing you."

"I guess you've already heard?"

"Good news travels fast. Bad news even faster," Glitter replied.

"What do the Feds have to do with this?"

"Now, Lou, you know better than me. Those guys are always sneaking around. Trying to pin something on me. I can tell you this. They got nothing. I run a legit business. It's a terrible thing about John. Had the highest collection of all the guys who worked for me. Good man. I was just leaving. I'm going to take a few days off. Don't want to be here when the questioning starts. No sense in making their job too easy."

"Where you headed?"

"Probably go to Detroit or Philly. Kind of let things cool down, if you know what I mean."

"Can you tell me about the man who went after John?" inquired Lou.

"Guy had a gambling problem. Had a lot of paper from the casinos in Tunica. I bought up a block for fifty cents on the dollar. John was just taking care of business."

Lou watched as Glitter get into the passenger side of a black BMW. The driver wore dark shades and a black leather ball cap. A gold chain hung outside his T-shirt. Lou pulled through the parking lot and headed downtown.

Parking his car in the lot along Riverside Drive, Lou strolled into the Beale Street District. The afternoon lunch crowds filled the sidewalks. The smell of grilling meats and frying potatoes lingered in the humid air. Several young black kids flipped in acrobat fashion for tips that were dropped into a glass jar. Music spilled onto the brick street. A guitarist sat on an outside barstool and picked the strings of B.B. King's 1951 "Three O'Clock Blues."

Lou had met Riley B. King, better known as B.B. King, several years earlier. B.B. had told Lou that he was born in 1925 near the town of Itta Bena, Mississippi, and that he started performing in the 1940s. King's cousin, Bukka White of Memphis, a well-known blues guitarist, had helped him create his own style based on the legendary performers of Blind Lemon Jefferson and T-Bone Walker. B.B. also told Lou about how years ago he had performed at the Sixteenth Avenue Grill in West Memphis. That had led to his ten-minute radio spots on WDIA, an all-black radio station in Memphis, under the name of Blues Boy King. The name was later shortened to B.B. King. Lou knew that B.B. King was hailed as the reigning king of the blues. Lou had seen him perform many times with his trademark Gibson guitar named Lucille.

"Lou, is that you?"

Lou stopped in front of A. Schwab's general store. Jim Damos and his wife, Esther, were exiting the store's glass doors. Esther was carrying a bulging nondescript plastic bag. A. Schwab opened in 1876, and was the oldest family-owned and operated general store in the mid-South. Three floors of clothes, rusty tools, Elvis souvenirs, and voodoo accessories shared their space with dusty toys and objects overflowing the painted wooden tables and shelves.

"Well, hi, Jim. How are you, Esther? Good to see you guys."

"I'm fine, Lou," she said.

"What brings you down here?"

"Esther and I still like to visit the old store. We used to shop here when our kids were growing up. I can't tell you how many pairs of blue jeans we bought from this store. The kids used to love coming here on Saturday. They would take all day deciding what kind of candy to get from the glass jars. Thought we might stop by the mission and see how things are going. I spent most of my life running that place. It's hard not to check on it every once in a while. How about you? Somehow, I don't get the feeling you're down here shopping."

"That's true. Just trying to follow up on a case."

"Is that the one the papers are calling the Memphis Mangler?" Esther asked. "It's just terrible that you haven't been able to find this person."

"Tell me about it. Captain Smitters is getting so much pressure from the mayor that he's pulling *my* hair out."

"Is there anything I can do to help?" asked Jim.

"Do you know a guy named Bill Lance? He works at the Tennessee Mental Health Center."

"Name sounds familiar. I haven't been down there for almost a year. What does he look like?" asked Jim.

"Big guy. Around six-foot-three, two hundred sixty pounds, salt-and-pepper short hair. Was in the army. Walks with a slight limp."

"I do remember him. I invited him to the mission once to help out with Thanksgiving dinners. Stayed with us all day. Helped clean up after it was all done. Seemed real genuine."

"Did he spend much time around the homeless?"

"He asked questions about some, and he wandered around the tables to see if they needed anything. You think he might be involved in the case somehow?"

"No, it's probably nothing. Just considering all avenues. You could do one thing for me, though."

"Sure, Lou. How can I help?"

"Maybe when you and Esther are down here, you could stop by the mission. Maybe talk to a few of the homeless. I know they feel comfortable talking to you. See if any of them have seen Bill Lance or anyone else hanging around the area. Right now, I'll take any information I can get."

"I can do that. Esther and I were heading down there now to see Pete Johnson. I'll do a little digging around. If I find out anything, I'll give you a call."

"Thanks, Jim. Good to see you again, Esther. Keep in touch."

"Come by and see us anytime." Esther leaned over and gave Lou a hug. "You look pretty exhausted. Are you taking care of yourself?"

"Just a little weather-beaten," replied Lou, rubbing his two-day-old beard.

"What you need is some of Esther's good old Southern cooking," said Jim. "You give us a call when you're going to be in Whitehaven. A good home-cooked meal will fix you right up."

"Thanks, I'll do that."

As soon as Jim and Esther were out of earshot, Lou called the precinct and gave instructions for a background check on Bill Lance. Crossing the street, he ordered a beer at one of the outside service windows. Gray clouds threatened in the afternoon sky. Pieces of trash bounced off the street as the wind gusted, a prelude to an approaching thunderstorm. The smell of dusty moisture became present in the warm air. Finishing a second beer, Lou pushed himself to take a walk down Cotton Row while there was still some light. Shadows stretched across the deserted street away from the Beale Street crowds. A bell could be heard from the Main Street Trolley as it stopped to announce its presence. A dark green car crossed Front Street on its way to the Beale Street District. A brown paper bag danced along the sidewalk and disappeared into an alley. Taking a deep breath, Lou followed the invitation.

The bag sat one-third of the way in, perched along a mound of trash, buffered from the wind. A few drops of rain spotted some broken glass windows in the alley. The walls of the adjacent buildings appeared to expand as they blocked out more of the overhead light. Lou felt a rush of adrenaline. His face flushed, and beads of sweat poured down his cheeks, mixing with the drops of rain. A flash of lightning exposed a human form standing beside one of the block-wall pilasters. Thunder ripped through the alley. Lou stood frozen, gasping for air. Lou's hands began to tremble. He felt light-headed, as if he was about to pass out. He was having trouble keeping his balance. Visions appeared in front of him.

A dark silhouette stepped out into the alleyway. Then another and another. Unable to support his shaking body, Lou crumbled to his knees. Rain poured over his body. A chill of cold air circled his head. Another flash of lightning seared the darkness. Sue was standing between two eyeless figures. A man jutted in front of the trio. Sue reached out to grab the man. A gunshot exploded. Lou covered his ears and screamed. A dark spot appeared in the neck area of Sue's white shirt and started to expand like ink on a blotter. She stared at Lou in shock. Her eyes fluttered and disappeared into her head. Another shot rang out. In less than a millisecond, Lou felt a bullet burn through his scalp and shatter his skull. His body twitched and fell forward onto the wet alley floor.

Lou jolted awake, startled and temporarily unsure of where he was. And then he remembered the visions, the light-headedness, and then blacking out. He didn't know how long he had been passed out, but the rain had stopped. The wet ground had penetrated all his clothes and left behind a cold chill. Pushing himself to his knees, he dared to look up. The dark alley was empty. Water dripped from a broken roof pipe and splashed into a puddle. Brown rings of water rippled to the edge. Feeling his pocket, he found his cell phone. His hands were shaking so much that he dropped the phone to the ground. Sweeping his hand across the wet alley, he picked up the phone and called Sue.

"Hi, Lou. What's up?"

Trying to control his breathing, Lou forced himself to speak.

"Are, are you okay?" Lou asked.

"I'm fine, but you sound like you're in trouble. Where are you? What's happened?"

Holding back his emotions as best he could, Lou took a deep breath.

"I'm good. Got to go. I'll call you tomorrow."

"Wait, I have some information on our mystery man from the market."

"Tomorrow. I'll call you tomorrow."

CHAPTER 7

Bones

JACK AND DAVE RECEIVED an emergency call and were dispatched to the Union Avenue Mission. Dispatch had told Jack that the caller identified himself as Pete Johnson. When they arrived, Pete was standing outside the front door of the mission. He hurried the policemen into the front entry and pointed to a note. Pete was very upset and not making a lot of sense.

"Slow down, Mr. Johnson, and start over again," insisted Jack.

"That was wedged behind the outside door handle of the entry door when I got here at 6:00 AM. It took me a minute to realize what I was holding. I dropped the note on the counter and immediately called the police." He wiped his hands on his pants.

Taking out his pen, Jack slipped the sheet of paper into a plastic bag and sealed the opening. Scribbled in black crayon was the message "Help, Bus." The handwriting was uneven and poorly printed.

Pacing the floor, Pete couldn't hold back anymore. "What does it mean? What bus? What's happened? Does this make any sense to you?"

Jack put his hand on Pete's shoulder and calmed him down. "Do you recognize the handwriting?"

"No, I don't think so. Not much there. Maybe. I don't know."

"Take a deep breath. Settle down. What about your sign-in book? Maybe there's something in there to help identify the writer."

"Not very many actually sign it themselves. Most just tell me their name, and I write it down, along with the date and time. I make some notes off to the side if I need to."

Turning the pages one by one, Jack spotted something that looked similar. The name Ted was written unevenly in all capital letters between two lines.

"Have you seen Ted lately?"

"No, not for a while. Maybe a week. I figured he had moved on. Most of the guys don't stay long."

"What makes you think he moved on?" Jack asked.

"Just haven't seen him around. That usually means a guy's left town."

"Has anyone been asking about him?"

"Just that detective. You know, that Cros guy."

"We're going to take this note and check it out. We'll be back in touch with you later today. If you need us, call direct. Do you still have my phone number?"

"Yes, I have it. I'll call if anything else happens."

Hurrying back to the patrol car, Jack headed toward the bus terminal.

"What are you thinking?" Dave asked.

"Don't know yet, but the note mentioned a bus. We need to check out the Greyhound Bus Terminal."

Pulling into the terminal parking lot, Jack and Dave left their car and walked toward the cyclone fence at the back of the lot. Several cars were parked in front of the building. Movement could be seen through the clouded glass front. The back lot was relatively empty. Sunlight was breaking over adjacent buildings, exposing puddles of water from the night's rain. A rusty car with a flat tire was parked on the side. No one was inside. The trunk was tied shut with a wire clothes hanger. Jack took out his flashlight and shined it between the gaps, noting that the trunk appeared empty. Inside, the floorboards were scattered with trash and coffee cups. Down a few spaces was a red pickup truck. The cab and bed were both empty. A Confederate flag hung inside the back window.

Around the back of the terminal was a banged-up green Dumpster with the side door and lid open. Approaching the Dumpster, Jack spotted a brown shoe lying on its side. Another step revealed the owner. An elderly white male lay next to the Dumpster, his body contorted. A dark string ran from the victim's forehead past his ear onto the damp pavement. The beam of Jack's flashlight displayed the crimson color of blood. Jack moved in and squatted down to get a closer look. The victim was in his fifties, approximately six feet tall, and weighed around one hundred forty pounds. His dirty clothes and unshaven face indicated that he was probably among the homeless population in Memphis. A gunshot wound to the head was obvious. Matted gray hair on the back of his head revealed the exit wound. Blood splatters and pieces of tissue hung on the top lip of the Dumpster. The Memphis Mangler had found his fourth victim. Being careful not to disturb the crime scene, Dave and Jack slowly backed away.

"Go ahead and tape this off while I call it in." Jack watched as Dave walked to the patrol car and removed a roll of yellow security tape. Taking a deep breath, Jack made a call to the police station. His second call was to Lou Cros.

The phone rang a third time. "Come on, Lou. Pick up the phone." The phone connected. Jack heard some fumbling with the phone on the line.

"Hello. This is Lou Cros." His voice was cracking and harsh.

"Lou, it's Jack. There's been another murder."

"Where are you?"

"Dave and I are at the Greyhound Bus Terminal. Sorry to wake you, but I wanted to give you a heads-up before you get a call from the captain. You don't sound good. You all right?"

"Yeah, I'm fine. What can you tell me?"

"Looks the same. One shot to the forehead. There's more. We got a tip that something was here from a note that was left at the mission. Looks like it could be Ted's handwriting. Nothing confirmed yet. I have the note in plastic."

"Give me a minute to clean up a bit, and I'll be on my way."

The sounds of sirens were already filling the moist air. Jack watched as Dave turned on the patrol car's rotating lights, drawing the immediate attention of those inside the terminal. A bald security guard with a scraggly beard exited the front doors and approached Jack. He appeared to be in his early thirties. His barreled belly stretched the buttons on his gray uniform shirt to near failure. Dark stains of sweat highlighted his armpits.

"What's going on?"

"There's been an incident in the back of the building. A man has been shot. I'd appreciate it if you would help out by keeping the people in the station for a few minutes until we can get their names and addresses. I don't want any buses to leave. My name is Jack Mills. My partner, Officer Dave Drake, will assist you. Can you do that?"

"Yeah, I can do that." The guard tugged on his belt. "Finally, some excitement."

"Excitement? You call a murder excitement? Don't you go anywhere, either. We definitely want to talk with you."

"Whatever, man." The security guard smiled and walked away.

Within minutes, the parking lot had three police cars, a special K-9 unit, and one that belonged to Paul Craft, the city's ME. Jack watched as a police dog was led into the terminal. He recognized this particular dog as one that was trained to sniff out gunpowder and other types of explosive material. The next car on the scene belonged to Lou, who had just pulled into the parking lot.

"What do we have so far?" Lou asked.

"Nothing yet," Jack said. "Doc and his team are going over the body. The K-9 unit is sniffing for any evidence of gunpowder in the suitcases inside. You need to check out the security guard. He is a real piece of work. Seemed happy that he has some excitement in his life. Everyone who was here when we arrived is still inside. No buses left."

"You still have the note?" asked Lou.

"It's right here. Glad to get rid of it," answered Jack.

"What makes you think it may have been written by Ted?"

"I looked through the sign-in book at the mission. Ted used all caps when he signed in. Looked similar. May or may not be his handwriting, but it sure looks similar."

The K-9 unit exited the terminal and approached the cars in the parking lot. Finding nothing that excited the dog, the K-9 officer headed to the Dumpster.

Lou entered the terminal and found eight people eager to leave the city. The bus driver stood at the counter alongside the security guard. Dave sipped from a cup of coffee he'd just bought at a vending machine and made a distasteful face.

"My name is Lou Cros. With one *S*. I'm an investigator for the Memphis Police Department. Has everyone given the officer your name, address, and where you can be reached?"

Most of the people nodded.

"Dave, do you have all the information?"

"Got it."

"I want to thank all of you for staying a little longer. We'll let you go shortly. Have you been told what has happened?"

A few more people nodded.

"Come on, people, speak up!" yelled the security guard. "We can't hear your head rattle!"

Lou turned and faced the guard. "And what might your name be?"

"Gary West," announced the guard, pushing his chest out.

"Well, Mr. West, I appreciate your eagerness, but I will handle this."

"Whatever."

"Dave, we'll also need any information you can get on the passengers that left last night or early this morning. Can you see what you can do?"

"I'll take care of it," Dave said.

"Now, did anyone see or hear anything while you were arriving or while you were inside?"

A couple of no's sounded out, along with a few headshakes.

"Anybody?" Lou asked. "Did anyone notice a car leaving the parking lot when they were arriving or notice any vehicles pulling out of the parking lot while you were inside?" Lou got the same response. "Okay, here's my card. If you think of anything that may help, please call."

"Load up, people," announced the security guard. "Time's a wastin'."

Lou approached Gary West for a second time. "Don't I know you?"

"Yeah, we met at South Memphis Pawn. You came in and threw your badge around."

"No, I don't think so. I've never been there. But I do know you from somewhere."

"Whatever."

"Are you still working at South Memphis Pawn?" Lou asked.

"Nope. Moved on. I'm at John's Pawnshop."

"John's Pawnshop. That's the one on Madison Avenue. I believe that John Henry is the brother of a man called Glitter. Is that right?"

"That's the place." Gary stroked his beard and smiled. Lou noticed the skull and crossbones tattooed on his right forearm.

"What are your hours at John's?"

"Eleven to eleven. Stop in and look around. Got some new stuff."

"So, how long have you been doing security?"

"Couple of years. Work part-time a few days a week. Helps with the ol' beer money. Know what I mean?"

"Where are you living?" continued Lou.

"Got a place near Winchester in Whitehaven. Not too far from Elvis's place."

Lou knew he was talking about the late Elvis Presley's Graceland Mansion, just south of Winchester on Elvis Presley Boulevard.

"I noticed your revolver. Looks like a .38 Ruger. Mind if I look at it?"

"Nope, help yourself." Taking the gun out of the holster, he handed it to Lou butt first.

Lou examined the barrel and smelled it to see if it had been fired recently. He then checked the chamber for a missing bullet.

"Looks like you take pretty good care of it. You do have a license to carry this?" Lou asked as he handed the gun back.

"You got to be kidding me? I work in a pawnshop from eleven to eleven, and you're asking me if I have a license? You got to be nuts, man."

"Yeah, I guess I am, but you didn't answer the question."

"I got a license. You happy now?"

"Whatever, man." Lou smiled, winked at Dave, and started to leave the terminal. "I remember now. I saw you at the Blue Monkey Bar and Grill. You had a Mohawk haircut then, and you were sitting with a guy named J. and a bunch of his friends. He called you Bones. So, you must know the fellow they call Boots. That right?"

"Yeah, I know 'im. So what?"

"You still hang out with those guys?" Lou asked.

"Not anymore. Heard the Feds busted them. I went my way, and they went theirs."

"That's kind of a strange tattoo. You ever ride with the Hell's Angels?"

"Like it?" Gary made a fist and held up his forearm to display the skull and crossbones artwork. "Got it one night in Voodoo Village."

"Yeah, that makes quite a statement," Lou said.

The police were very familiar with Voodoo Village. Lou remembered it being a fenced-in compound located at the dead end of Mary Angela Road in south Memphis. Over the years, there had been reports of animal sacrifice rituals there, much like African voodoo. It was considered one of the haunted places of Memphis, and it often inspired high school Friday or Saturday night dares. For some, going there at night was a rite of passage.

"You guys need me for anything else?" asked the guard.

"Nothing right now, but I'm sure we'll talk further," said Lou.

"Whatever."

Lou exited the building and found Jack leaning against his patrol car. Besides the ME and the crime scene team, the rest of the police had left.

"How did you like that security guard?" asked Jack, shaking his head in disbelief.

"I can see why the crime rate in this city is so high. It'll give any fruitcake a license to carry a gun. I'll have the office check him out. You never know what they might find."

"Doc said the temperature of the body puts time of death around 2:00 AM," said Jack. "He's taking the body back to the lab."

"Thanks for the heads-up. I'm surprised that I haven't gotten that call from Smitters yet."

Dave left the building and hooked up with Lou and Jack. "Here's a copy of the names and addresses that will be in the report." Dave handed a sheet of paper to Lou. "Not much help. Only three people paid with credit cards. The others paid with cash. Nobody saw or heard anything. The loudmouthed guard said he was sitting by the bus door entrance most of the night. Didn't see or hear anything. The bus driver who was there grinned and shook his head. It would be my guess that the guard was either sleeping in the back or sitting in the break room."

"Thanks, Dave. What about the car with the flat over there? Did you find out who owns it?" Lou referred the question to Jack.

"Belongs to a custodian who works here," Jack said. "I spoke to him on the phone. He said the terminal manager told him he had to haul it off. Just hasn't gotten around to it yet. The pickup truck—"

"What a minute! Let me guess. It belongs to the security guard," said Lou, breaking out in a laugh.

"You got it!"

Lou's cell phone began ringing. Looking at the caller ID, he held the phone up for Jack to see.

"Glad it's you and not me," smiled Jack.

"Yes, Captain. What can I do for you?"

"Cros, you better have some good news for me. The mayor's office has already called. The Feds are outside my office. I can't hold them off much longer."

"I got a couple of leads I need to follow up on. I just need a few more days, and I'll have something for you." Lou gritted his teeth as he spoke.

"A few more days! Forty-eight hours, Lou. That's all I can give you unless you bring me some hard evidence. What we need is an arrest."

"Forty-eight hours? Come on, Captain, I can't work miracles. Tell them we have some real leads in this case, and that if they step in now, it will cause a setback in the investigation."

"Give me something, Lou. I need something!"

"Tell them we need an extra two days to follow up on some out-of-town leads. Come on, Captain, help me here."

"I'll give the mayor a call and see what I can do. He owes me one. But you'd better not be lying to me. I'll have your badge on this one."

"You won't be disappointed. I'm all over it."

"I'll get you the four days, but you better bring me something. Four days. That's all you have."

"Got it. Now let me get back to work."

Lou closed his phone and took a deep breath. Jack gave him a questioning look.

"Captain says he can get me four days to bring him some hard evidence, or the Feds are taking over."

The three men were distracted from their conversation as the sound of a zipper screeched against a plastic bag. From his vantage point, Lou saw the medical team putting the closing touches on the body.

"I'll see you guys later. I want to talk to Doc before he leaves."

Jack and Dave remained by the patrol car. Lou approached the yellow security tape.

"Any news, Doc?"

"Hi, Lou. Looks pretty much like the same MO. One shot to the front of the skull. No ligature marks on his wrists or ankles. I'd put TOD at around 2:00 AM. No defensive wounds on his hands or knuckles. I'd say he was standing just in front of the Dumpster when he was shot. Bullet exited the back of his head and lodged in the lip of the Dumpster. We'll have to check the weight of the fragment when we get back to the lab. Powder burns on the face indicate the gun was about six to eight inches away from his head when the killer fired it. Something is wedged in the back of the victim's throat. I'll get it out back at the lab."

"Thanks, Doc. Please give me a call once you finish the autopsy."

"Sure, Lou. It will probably be within the next couple of hours. The mayor's office called and wants me to put it on the top of my list. The team is dusting the Dumpster and will go through the container to see if anything shows up."

"Thanks, Doc. I'll talk to you later."

Lou strolled around the back parking lot. Puddles of water spotted the cracked and uneven asphalt. Newspapers and Styrofoam cups hugged the cyclone fence that encircled the terminal. No footprints or car tracks were visible. A gust of wind whistled through the fence and picked up some debris, whirling it around into a small tornado. A piece of the paper broke loose from the little whirlwind and pinned itself against Lou's chest. Grabbing the paper, he started to toss it aside, but something caught his eye. He felt himself quiver as he stared at the Big Red gum wrapper.

It was midmorning when Lou got his call from Paul Craft. Doc was able to confirm several items that were critical to the investigation. It was a .38-caliber round that had splintered the homeless man's skull. What little barrel marking could be seen from the flattened bullet indicated that the murder weapon was probably the same gun used in the other murders, but that couldn't be confirmed. The angle of trajectory from the entry and exit wound, along with the fragment in the Dumpster lip, put the shooter's height between five foot six and five foot eight. No sexual abuse marks were found. Nothing under his fingernails to indicate a struggle. No unusual bruising on his body. There was also a piece of fresh chewing gum lodged in the victim's throat. Pete Johnson and Jim Damos had been called in to see if they could identify the body. There was no ID at the present time.

Lou sat in the parking lot of John's Pawnshop. The morning murder kept running through his mind. A rapid succession of thoughts troubled him. *A lot of people chew gum. Might be the victim's gum. Could be anybody's. Sure, Sue chews Big Red, but so do I. Doesn't mean anything. I'll give her a call later. Forget the gum. Find the shooter. That's what I need to concentrate on.*

The parking lot of John's Pawnshop was empty except for a blue BMW. Entering the barred door, Lou approached the black man behind the counter. Stereos and VCRs lined the metal shelves on both sides. A couple of guitars and three brass horns hung on the back wall. A long glass counter filled with jewelry, handguns, and knives separated the back wall from the front of the store. Cameras hung from the ceiling on both sides.

"Name is Lou Cros. Looking for Gary West."

The man behind the counter looked Lou over and hesitated before he spoke. "You must be that cop my brother told me about. My name is John Henry. I own this shop."

"Nice to meet you, John. You heard from Glitter? When is he due back?"

"Probably today. He said he wouldn't be gone but two days. What can I do for you?"

"Looking for Gary West. Is he working today?"

"Don't work here no more. Cut him loose three days ago."

"Well, that's strange. I spoke with him this morning, and he said he worked for you."

"Can't help you with that. Man don't work here no more."

"Could you share with me why not?"

"Yeah, the guy's an idiot. Came to work with a Confederate flag in the back of his truck. How long do you think he will live doing something stupid like that? Man's a few bricks short. I sent him packing."

"Did you have any trouble with him while he was here?"

"Just his mouth. Mouthed off too much. Acted like he owned the place. Made some of my customers real mad. He wasn't good for business. Glad to get rid of him."

"Did any of his friends ever come by?"

"Couple of times. You know the type. All dressed up in black with funky hairdos."

"You ever hear their names?"

"Can't help you there. Never bought anything. Didn't pay much attention to them."

"Thanks, John." Lou handed him one of his cards.

"Don't need no card. If something comes up, Glitter will get in touch."

Leaving the store, Lou checked the address list from Dave and headed toward the Whitehaven Apartments on Elvis Presley Boulevard. Pulling into the back of the apartments, Lou verified Gary West's apartment number. The red truck was parked along the back wooden fence. Climbing three flights of concrete stairs, Lou banged on the door of apartment 303. Two minutes passed. No answer. Lou banged again.

"All right! Hold on!" shouted a familiar voice from inside. The door chain rattled against the frame. The door banged open as it stuck against the jam. Gary West stood in a small kitchen area in his boxer shorts. His large stomach protruded over the waistband. A tattoo of a two-headed snake was etched into the left side of his chest. His unruly beard was pushed to one side.

"What the hell you want? I'm trying to get some sleep here!"

"You lied to me this morning. You told me you worked at John's Pawnshop. John said he fired you several days ago. This is a murder investigation. I can lock you up for that."

"I never said that!" he shouted back. "You got it wrong!"

"I don't think so. You told me you worked from eleven to eleven. Now I need some real answers."

"You got it wrong, man. I said I used to work at the shop. You need to clean your ears out. Now get the hell out of here and leave me alone before I sue you for harassment."

Gary started to shut the door, but Lou stuck his foot across the threshold.

"You're in my territory now!" yelled Gary, pulling the door back open and taking a swing at Lou's face.

Lou took a glancing blow to the side of his head. Catching himself against the doorjamb, he delivered a powerful forearm to Gary's face, knocking him over on his back. Gary tried to roll over on his side to get back on his feet, but Lou stomped on his shoulder and pinned him down on the floor again. Grabbing Lou's ankle, Gary shoved him against the stove and tried again to regain his feet. Pushing himself off the stove, Lou directed the heel of his shoe straight into Gary's temple. Gary's head slapped the linoleum floor. His body went limp.

Lou wiped the sweat from his face and dragged Gary into the living room. The apartment smelled of stale beer and cigarettes. Trash and empty beer cans littered the coffee table. Two pieces of pizza with a fuzzy green growth sat on a paper plate. Black cigarette burn craters speckled the green couch. A picture of Adolf Hitler and a swastika hung in a frame above the rabbit-ear TV. Glancing into the bedroom, Lou saw more of the same. Empty beer bottles, clothes spread across the floor, and ashtrays full of cigarette butts. A gun rack was hanging from two large screws. An M-4 assault rifle with scope and a sawed-off double-barreled shotgun were chained and padlocked in the rack. A holster and the same .38-caliber handgun he had seen earlier at the bus terminal were next to an open gun case on top of a chest of drawers. The Ruger, a model 100 double-action revolver with a four-inch barrel, struck Lou as odd. It was the kind of gun ideal for packing while wearing a suit. This guy didn't look like he'd worn a suit in all his life. Lou figured this idiot for a semiautomatic kind of guy. Maybe a Glock guy, or maybe even the kind of guy who would favor an Uzi set on full automatic.

Quickly searching the drawers, Lou found half a dozen gold chains, several gold rings, two hunting knives, and a set of brass knuckles. The bed and closet revealed a stun gun, a deer rifle with scope, a .22-caliber rifle, and five small bags of marijuana. Using his phone camera, Lou took pictures of all the items. Taking the stun gun back into the living room, he pulled a chair up alongside Gary and waited.

Regaining consciousness, Gary slowly rubbed the side of his head and pushed himself to a sitting position. Squinting his eyes, he looked up to see his incarcerator.

Lou pressed the trigger on the stun gun. Jagged lines of electricity bounced between the two electrodes. The crackling sound got Gary's full attention.

"You ever felt one of these? We had to stun each other in the academy. The pain feels like a thousand hot nails shooting through your body. You begin to spasm, and most people pass out. Some lose control of their body functions. Not a pretty sight at all. If I were you, I'd stay right where you are."

"You're crazy, man! You broke into my place! You got nothing on me!" Gary yelled.

"I guess you could file a complaint if you want, but I might need to spread around some of the pictures I have."

Opening his phone, Lou turned the screen at an angle so Gary could see.

"Let's see. Here's a good one of an assault rifle and a sawed-off shotgun. The Feds might want to know if you have papers on these."

"Those are all legal, man!"

"Maybe, but I'm sure they would like to check that out. And here is another good one. John Henry might like to know where this jewelry came from. Now this one is my favorites—just a few little nickel bags of weed. That should get you off the street for a while."

"What do you want, man?"

"Just some straight answers. The fellow you call Boots was at Huey's on South Second Street one night with a bunch of his cronies. They got thrown out, and they apparently pushed a homeless guy around on the street when they left. Were you there that night?"

"Yeah, so what?"

"That homeless guy ended up dead that night. So, what can you tell me about that night?"

"Nothing, man. Boots pushed the guy around a little, and that was it. The guy shuffled off, and we went to Silky's for a beer."

"Did any of the guys split and go somewhere else?"

"No, man. We all went to Silky's."

"Did you see anyone following the guy when he left?"

"No, but another homeless guy kind of met up with him. You know, like those guys do?"

"Which way were they going?"

"Down toward the river."

"What did the other guy look like?"

"He was a homeless guy, man! They don't look like anything!"

"Did he have a hat on? Maybe a coat? How tall was he? Was he carrying anything? You must have seen something."

"He was a homeless guy, man! They all look the same. Can I get up now?"

"Not just yet. This morning you told me that you don't run with those guys anymore."

"Yeah, that's right."

"You're a terrible liar. John Henry said that two of them came by the shop to see you. So, which is it?"

"Those guys are just a couple of young punks looking to get something for nothing. I told them to get lost."

Lou stood up and tossed the stun gun on the couch. Pulling the chair out of Gary's reach, he headed for the back door.

"Hey, man. You were just kidding about the Feds, right? I mean I told you everything I know."

Taking out one of his cards, Lou dropped it on top of the stove. "We'll see. Call me if you remember anything else. Maybe I'll forget what I saw."

"Come on, man, give me a break. I'm telling you, I don't know nothing about that homeless guy."

"I'll think about it. Call me if you remember anything."

Lou headed out the door. When he reached his car, he called Sue. He needed to update her on the fourth victim and to get any information she had on Cotton and the man from the market. The gum in the victim's throat popped into his mind again. Maybe he would leave that information out for now. Something wasn't right. He needed to sort things out in his mind.

CHAPTER 8

The Mangler

THE LATE AFTERNOON SUN seared the red brick paving of the Beale Street District. Shadows of parapet walls fell from building tops and inched along the concrete sidewalks. Visible waves of heat escaped the pavement only to be reabsorbed in the surrounding humid air. Head-bobbing pigeons strutted between the foot traffic and fought over morsels of food that dropped from above. Specks of dust climbed the rays of evening sunlight and slowly disappeared overhead. Smells of cooking meat and seafood gumbo were obvious at nearly every open door. Blaring music drowned out the occasional loud laughing that came from small pockets of people on the street.

"What was that call about?" inquired Dave.

"That was Cros," replied Jack. "The background noise sounds like he's in a bar somewhere. Can you believe that guy? Here we are working twelve-hour shifts, and he wants us to stay over tonight and meet with him at nine. Says he thinks the Mangler could be a homeless person or someone dressing up like a homeless person."

"Yeah, well, you seem irritated. What else is going on?"

"Just burns me up. Here he is acting like a booze head and not returning calls, and he wants us to put in fourteen or fifteen hours because he can't stomach the pressure anymore? He should've retired when he had the chance. He doesn't seem the same as before. He's edgy and not in control. I mean

I love the guy, but he could've told us whatever he needed to tell us on the phone, or he could've gotten his lazy butt out of the bar and met us on our beat."

"Jack, don't forget we're all working for the same reason. We've got a serial killer on the streets. I know you. You'll work twenty-four a day if you think it'll help find this guy."

Jack took a deep breath and calmed himself down. "You're right. It was just the way he said it. It was more demanding than asking. Forget what I said. I guess I'm getting a little cranky in my old age. I mean, it's not like I have a black-tie event to go to."

Passing the open door of the Blues City Café, Dave stopped and inhaled the savory aroma of grilling steaks. "Man that smells good. I'm getting hungry. How about you?"

"Yeah, I could use a bite. What you got in mind?" Jack said.

"How about some catfish and gumbo?"

"What, no deep-fried hamburger? You must be feeling sick," Jack teased.

"Maybe later."

Ordering from the café street window, Jack looked over the crowds.

"Dave, over there by B.B. King's, isn't that the security guard from the Greyhound Bus Terminal?"

"That's him. Name is Gary West."

"He's standing around like he's waiting for someone."

Gary made eye contact with the two officers. He quickly turned and disappeared into the crowd.

"You want to follow him?" asked Dave.

"No, let's give him some space and see who he hooks up with."

The officers watched as Gary West ducked into the Rum Boogie Café.

Gary West took a seat at a corner table and ordered a beer. Touching the small bag of marijuana in his pants pocket, he took out his cell phone and sent a text message. "Will contact later. Break off."

Another customer entered the café and sat at the bar. Gary noticed that he walked around several chairs before taking his seat. After another beer, Gary looked back at the man seated at the bar. The man was watching him in a Budweiser mirror hanging on the wall. When they made eye contact, the man at the bar dropped his head, threw some money on the counter, and left the café. The man was wearing an oversized tie-dyed T-shirt and black jeans. Gary noticed his snakeskin boots.

Lou ordered another rum and Coke. Lifting his glass to get the last few drops, his hand began to tremble. Setting the glass back down on the scarred wooden tabletop, he grabbed it with both hands. The muscles in his forearms contracted, and he felt a spark of electricity flow through his body. It wasn't an unpleasant feeling, more like warm water being injected into his veins. His pulse quickened, and he immediately felt dizzy. A drop of sweat ran down the side of his face and fell on his shirt collar. His thoughts went to Sue.

Sue was sitting across from him at a high bar table. The round tabletop supported a half-eaten pepperoni pizza and several empty bottles of beer. She was laughing at one of his jokes and tilting her head to one side. Her hair was long and pulled through the back of a white CSI baseball cap. She looked perfect in every way. He remembered feeling strong and confident. Sue made eye contact a little longer than normal, blushed, and turned away. Glancing back, she started to say something and then hesitated.

"What? What were you about to say?"

"Probably something I will be sorry for," she responded as she tried to laugh it off.

"Try me."

"It's just that I really enjoy being with you."

"Stop right there. I don't like the way that started. It sounds like a but statement. I don't handle buts very well."

Sue looked away again. "Just bad timing."

For one of the few times in his life, Lou struggled for a witty reply and ended up saying nothing. The lion became the lamb.

Coming out of his reverie, Lou felt the failure of an opportunity missed and the loneliness of his existence. Looking down at his empty glass, he considered himself a broken man. Lately, nothing seemed to be going his way. The investigation was going nowhere, and for the first time in his career, he felt overwhelmed.

Jack and Dave finished their twelve-hour shift without incident. Agreeing to meet back at the Hard Rock Café at nine, they grabbed a couple hours of rest before they returned to the Beale Street District. Sitting at one of the outside wrought-iron tables, they both ordered a glass of sweet tea. After two unanswered phone calls from Jack, Lou showed up at 9:25 PM. His appearance was sloppy, and his clothes were wrinkled. A small red knot pushed out of his right cheekbone from the earlier encounter with Gary West.

Dave jumped in to cut off Jack's obvious irritation. "So, what's this all about?"

"I just wanted to bring you guys up to date. We only have a few days left before the Feds take over. I paid a visit to Gary West, a.k.a. Bones, the security guard from the Greyhound Bus Terminal."

"Is that where your mouse came from?" Dave asked, referring to the knot on Lou's cheekbone.

"Yeah, he decided to try to take me out. His mistake. Didn't work out. Anyway, he told me he was at Huey's the night the homeless guy was murdered. Said he saw another homeless person follow the victim out of the Beale Street District. I think he knows more than he's telling. He may be able to ID the guy."

"So, what are you saying?" asked Dave.

"We may be looking for another homeless person or someone who is dressing up like one in order to get accepted. Another thing is that the handwriting on the bus note was checked out, and there is a very high possibility that the writer is Ted. I believe he's the key to this investigation. I've put out a BOLO. We need to pick him up for questioning."

Lou ran his right hand through his hair, stifled a yawn, and paused for a moment, letting the conversation stop while he collected his thoughts. Then he said, "There's another guy that you need to be looking out for. His name is Bill Lance. He works at the Tennessee Mental Health Center. He has had contact with the mission and some of the homeless men. The captain pulled a picture ID from the army's information database."

Lou handed Dave a folded-up piece of paper with the information. "He's a military hero from Desert Storm. Big man. Walks with a slight limp. I'd just like to know if he shows up anywhere."

Jack leaned forward in his chair and spoke for the first time. "Lou, we're going to do all we can to help. But let me be real clear. We've been working twelve-hour shifts for the past week, six days a week." Jack held up his hand as Dave tried to step in to soften what was coming. "As I was saying—Jack gave Dave one of those looks before he returned to Lou—"the next time you call us from a bar and ask us to meet you after hours, we're going to have a heart-to-heart. This is not all about Lou. And don't deny you were in a bar because I could hear the music in the background. Am I clear?"

Lou stared at Jack for a minute. A big grin spread over his face. "Now, that's the Jack I know. Point taken. Guilty as charged."

Totally disarmed, Jack leaned back in his chair.

"West was here earlier, at around five," Dave said, trying to lighten the conversation. "And he appeared to be waiting for someone. Once he saw us, he slipped out. Don't know if he's still down here or not."

"Any homeless on the street?" asked Lou.

"Haven't seen any," replied Dave.

"One other thing. You guys know Jim Lovell?"

"Yeah, I know him. He works as an undercover agent, doesn't he?" asked Jack.

"Right. He'll be on the street as a homeless person. He'll be wearing an Atlanta Braves ball cap and will be staying at the mission. Street name will be Matt."

"Anything else?" asked Dave.

"No, that's it. I'm going to hang out here for a while longer. I'll give you a call if something shows up."

Jack and Dave finished their teas and headed for home. Lou sat at the table and took in the nightly music. Within a few minutes, he spotted Gary West. West was by himself, and he appeared to be annoyed with a young couple on the street. He was talking loudly and waving his arms in an intimidating manner. Two men stepped in to assist the young couple. Seeing himself outnumbered, West dropped a few choice words and backed off. Stepping off the curb, he lost his balance and spilled his beer. Crushing the empty cup in his hand, he threw it into the street. Crowds of people seemed to divide as he staggered through them. Looking down the street, West made eye contact with Lou. Hesitating for a minute, he turned away and headed off in the other direction. After another twenty minutes, Lou decided to take a walk through the district and then head home for the night.

The crowds on the streets started to thin out, and the street cleaners moved through the district picking up the trash that had accumulated during the evening. Leaving Beale Street from the east side, Lou walked through an alley to the coin-operated parking lot where he was parked. Passing a garbage Dumpster in the alley, he heard something moving toward him. Unable to react, he felt the pressure of an object strike the side of his head. The sound of breaking glass echoed off the walls. Crumbling to the pavement, Lou felt a sharp kick to his rib cage. In his dazed state, Lou looked up to see his attacker.

Gary West stood over his motionless body and pitched the broken end of a beer bottle toward the Dumpster. "Now we're even, man." Gary spit on Lou and delivered one more kick to Lou's midsection before he walked away. Lou lost consciousness.

The Mangler moved through the shadows of the Beale Street District and headed down toward the safety of Cotton Row. The crowds had died down. The last two open bars in the area had closed. The streetlights along Riverside Drive gave little illumination to the shadowed parking areas. Dots of headlights crossed the Hernando DeSoto Bridge and danced off the flowing waters of the muddy Mississippi River. Fireflies flickered at ground level, trying to impress a mate. The crescent moon peeked out from a black cloud and then disappeared.

The Mangler continued through the alleyways, staying in the hidden protection of the buildings. Crouching down behind a broken wooden fence, the Mangler surveyed the surroundings. A small mouse stuck its head out from under a piece of rotting timber. The Mangler watched as the mouse raised its head to sniff the night air. Both remained perfectly still, as if playing a game of move-first-and-lose. Faces of people flashed through the Mangler's mind. Some of the faces were covered in blood, while others were distorted and elongated with terrified looks of shock.

The Mangler approached the lone truck. A Confederate flag was stretched across the back window. A sleeping man sat behind the wheel. The driver's side window was down. The Mangler pressed the muzzle of his .38-caliber Smith & Wesson model 10 against Gary West's temple. Opening his eyes for a split second, Gary viewed his assailant. His body jerked as the gun discharged. His disfigured head slammed against the front seat. Dark splatters of blood polka-dotted the truck's interior. The Mangler grinned and slipped away.

CHAPTER 9

Matt

THE UNDERCOVER MOLE SAT on a cot inside the Union Avenue Mission. His worn tennis shoes and frayed blue jeans supported his disguise as a homeless man. Spaced around the room were fourteen cots. The large open area could easily accommodate ten or twelve more beds. Five restrooms aligned the back wall, along with a shower room that had eight partitioned stalls. A small room used by the janitor was to the right. At midmorning, the cot room was empty, with the exception of one man in the back corner. Matt took off his cap and wiped his fingers through his stringy hair. He made eye contact for a split second with the man in the corner before the tenant turned his back on him and pulled himself into a fetal position on the cot.

An elderly white man exited the shower room with a bucket and mop and surveyed the surroundings. Taking little notice of Matt, he started his daily cleanup. Working his way toward Matt, the man stopped short and looked at the floor where Matt's feet were stationed. Slowly bringing his eyes up, he faced Matt for the first time. The man appeared to be in his seventies, of medium build with white patches of curly hair planted over his ears and around the back of his head. He had a small scar down the right side of his mouth. Matt picked up his feet and stretched his slender body just inside the six-foot metal bed frame.

"Name's Matt," he said in a low voice.

"They call me Cotton. Guess my real name don't matter no more. Got to think real hard to remember it myself. First time here?"

"Yeah, just looking for a friend who said he was staying here. How is it here?" Matt asked.

"Pretty good, really. Pete Johnson runs this place now. You probably met him when you came in. Beds are clean, and the food is eatable. Expect to stay long?"

"Nope, just passing through. How about you?"

"Wife passed away several years ago. I got to drinking and lost everything else I had. Fellow used to work here by the name of Jim Damos picked me up and helped me get clean. Been working here ever since. Helping out keeps me from feeling sorry for myself. You on the booze?"

"No, not me. Just a string of bad luck. Going down to Mississippi to some family. They got a small farm there. Looking for some honest work," Matt said.

"Talk with Pete. He has some jobs available for those who want to work. Be enough to tide you over."

"Yeah, thanks. I will. I need to find my friend first. You know of a guy named Ted? He said I could meet him here."

Cotton looked around the room to be sure the other man wasn't listening and leaned down. "Man, the whole city is looking for him. Even had a detective asking a bunch of questions."

"You didn't tell him anything, did ya?"

"No way. We stick together around here. Ted ain't done nothing. They say they want him for questioning. Mark my words, there's more to it than that," Cotton said.

"How do you know?"

"I saw Ted about two weeks ago. Said someone was following him. Said he didn't feel safe here. Said somebody tried to kill him."

"Man, the sooner I can find him, the quicker we can get out of here. Know how I can find him?"

Cotton started to speak but pulled back. "No, can't say I do."

"Well, if you see him, tell him Matt is waiting for him."

"I'll do that." Cotton picked up his mop and continued moving around the room.

Matt stretched back out on the cot and lowered his Atlanta Braves baseball cap over his eyes. "Tell him I'm not going to stay here long, so if he wants to go with me, he'd best let me know."

Cotton nodded and continued working. "If I see him, I'll tell him."

Cotton finished straightening up and rolled the mop bucket to the doorway leading to the front office. Leaning forward, he yelled into the hallway. "Pete, the floor is drying. I'm going to take me a break and finish up cleaning when it dries. I'll be back in my room if you need me."

"Okay, nothing going on here. Take your time," Pete said.

Returning to the janitor's room, Cotton opened the fuse box and unscrewed one of the fuses. The red light on the emergency exit door alarm turned black. Peeking out the doorway, he checked to see if Matt was still down. Convinced Matt wasn't watching, Cotton picked up a small backpack and exited through the fire door in the back of the building. Looking up at the midday sun, he squinted his eyes, threw the pack over one shoulder, and left the back alley. Matt heard the metal door shut and quickly responded.

Cotton zigzagged through a couple of alleyways and ended up at the east entry of the Peabody Hotel. Entering the double glass doors, he lingered in the atrium area, looking over his shoulder. Feeling safe, Cotton left through the north doors and turned toward the river. Crossing the trolley car tracks at Main Street, he proceeded to the Cotton Row District. Arriving at Confederate Park, he sat on the jagged rampart stone wall overlooking the river bluff. Placing the backpack next to him, he waited.

A small boy was running between the towering oaks and hiding from his mother. She slipped around the trunk and surprised him. The boy broke out in laughter and took off running to start the game anew. Cotton watched as an elderly couple stood in front of the Jefferson Davis Memorial. The sign over the Memorial read, "President of the Confederate States of America 1861–1865." Several pedestrians walked along the sidewalk that separated the park from the street. The giant oaks made themselves known as the sound of the green leaves replied to the gentle winds. The peaceful sound reminded Cotton of his time as a young boy in north Memphis, sitting under the greenery of a backyard willow tree.

A tap on the stone wall broke into his memory. Crouching behind the wall, Ted pulled Cotton back to the present. Opening his backpack, Cotton took out a bottle of water and two sandwiches and slid them to Ted.

"There is a man at the mission says you and him were supposed to travel to Mississippi together. Says his name is Matt."

"Don't know any Matt. You tell him anything?" Ted asked.

"No, nothing. He asked a lot of questions. Said he needed to find you. You sure you don't know him? How'd he know you were heading to Mississippi?"

"Don't know him. You sure he didn't follow you?"

"Yeah, I'm sure. You better stay low for a few more days. I hear they got the police watching the roads out of here."

"Thanks, Cotton. We better not meet here anymore," Ted said.

"You going to be okay?" Cotton asked.

"I'll be okay."

"I'll leave some food in the back alley of the mission under a mop bucket. If you need anything, let me know. You sure you'll be okay?"

"I'm good."

The meeting lasted less than a minute. Cotton stood up, threw the backpack over his shoulder, and left the park.

Matt, who was across the street, witnessed the meeting between Cotton and a man he believed might be Ted. From the distance and with the stone wall blocking some of his vision, it was hard to tell. He had to make a quick decision. Should he storm at the two men and blow his cover, or should he wait for a better opportunity? He chose the latter. He quickly found his way back to the mission in order to beat Cotton's entrance. Once inside, he lay down on his cot and covered his eyes with his cap. Everything was the same as when he left.

Within a minute or two, he heard the back door open and close. Footsteps sounded on the floor. Matt turned over on his side, as if the sound had disturbed him. Cotton looked over at the two men in the room, retrieved the mop bucket, and disappeared into the back room. Matt waited five more minutes and walked through the hallway to the front entrance. Pete Johnson was at the front desk reading a book.

"I'm going to get some fresh air."

"Sure, Matt," Pete said, looking up from his book. "Just sign out before you leave."

Matt signed the book, exited the mission, and headed straight for Cotton Row. Walking along Front Street, he looked down every alleyway for signs of Ted. About halfway down the street, Matt saw an overhead shadow move across the dirty alley. Glancing up, he noticed a third-floor emergency door ajar on a rusting fire escape ladder. As he watched, the door slowly closed. Approaching the bottom of the ladder, he uprighted an old shelf unit and started his ascent. Sticking his finger in the hole once filled with the door handle, Matt opened the door and slid inside.

The afternoon sun broke through the dirty windows, exposing the sample room. Two cotton snake tables ran the length of the room. Scattered pieces of ceiling plaster and dust spotted the painted black-wood table surfaces. Empty plastic water bottles and sheets of collapsed corrugated boxes filled the inside corner of the room. Footprints covered the dusty floor. Staying close to the inside walls to avoid loose and squeaky floor slats, Matt quietly moved toward the office door. When he peered through the frosted door sidelight window, he saw a dark figure moving along the back wall. Pushing the door open, he found that the room was empty. The front office door was ajar. An empty bottle of water and small paper bag were on the floor. Footprints dotted the dust toward the front office door.

Matt quickly exited through the front door to a hallway. To his left, he heard footsteps running down the stairwell. The sound of a door slamming echoed through the building. Matt rushed down the dusty stairs and searched the lower level. Nothing. He stood still and listened for any sound that might give him some hope. The building was silent. Totally frustrated, he leaned against the wall.

"Damn!"

CHAPTER 10

The Confession

LOU ORDERED A BLACK coffee at the Union Avenue Burger King. The news of Gary West's murder kept running through his mind. West was in the area on the night the first homeless man was murdered. West also admitted to seeing someone following the victim out of the Beale Street area. Maybe West knew too much. Or, maybe it was like the police reported, a drug deal gone bad.

Making his way to the back of the restaurant, Lou spotted Glitter sitting in a booth in the back corner. He was wearing a pair of white sunglasses and a white silk shirt. Several gold chains hung around his neck, along with his signature *G* chain. Across from him was a dark-featured Hispanic-looking man. He had short-cropped dark hair and a tiny one-inch-wide beard that extended from his sideburns to a small patch of whiskers on his chin. A navy blue sleeveless Terminator T-shirt accentuated his muscular arms and shoulders. Not waiting for an invitation, Lou slid into the booth next to him.

"Well, Detective Lou Cros, as I live and breath," said Glitter with a snicker.

"Hi, Mr. G. How was your trip?" asked Lou.

"Good. Everything was good." Glitter pulled his sunglasses down a bit on his nose and peered over the white frame to better view the scratches on Lou's face. "Looks like you've had a little excitement since I've been gone."

"Some. Nothing I couldn't handle. Aren't you going to introduce me to your new friend?" Lou glanced over at the man next to him.

"Well, forgive me," Glitter said, putting on an apologetic air. "Rocky here was just telling me a little about himself. I'm just doing some interviews right now. He was just leaving. Push out and let the man out."

Lou slid out as Rocky removed himself from the booth.

"I'll get back with you," Glitter said, smiling at Rocky.

Rocky nodded and left the restaurant.

"Where'd you meet him?" asked Lou.

"Walked in off the street. Said he heard I was looking for a collector."

"Did he say where he heard that?"

"Nope. Too tight-lipped for me. Usually means they're hiding something. I don't hire people without references. Don't need any trouble. This one smells of trouble."

"Have you heard anything new about the Mangler?" Lou asked.

"No, a little too early yet. Just got back in town last night. I know this, though. New information is going to get expensive," Glitter said and grinned. "Probably cost you a C-note. I do know that the cops got it wrong on that guy who used to work for my brother."

"You're talking about Gary West?"

"That's him."

Lou thought for a few moments. He leaned back in the seat, and then decided to go into some detail for Glitter, hoping it might prompt him to provide more information. He said, "The investigation report doesn't fit with the Mangler. First, it was a different MO. Second, the bullet exited through the truck's back window and was never found, so no ballistics could be run. Third, since the victim was in possession of a large amount of cash and some marijuana, it appeared to be a drug buy or sale that had gone wrong. And fourth, the last cell phone number that was called turned out to be that of a drug user who had been busted for several misdemeanors in the past year. The drug user was picked up and questioned, but was able to produce the text message that he had saved on his phone. He also had several witnesses who vouched for his whereabouts that night."

"Come on, Lou. If that was a drug killing, I'm the King of Siam. West was a lowlife, but he wasn't a pusher. Besides, he had money and marijuana on him when he was found. That sound like a drug deal to you? You don't shoot a man and then leave your goods behind. That don't make any sense. No, sir, that was just someone getting even. That man had a lot of enemies. If I hear anything, I'll give you a call."

"Thanks, Mr. G." Lou took out a twenty-dollar bill and dropped it on the table. "Buy yourself a cup of coffee."

Glitter pushed the money back to Lou. "Today is on me. The next one will cost big-time."

Picking up the money, Lou bumped knuckles with Glitter and left the restaurant. Taking out his phone, Lou gave Sue a call. When she answered and they said hi, he asked, "Where are you?"

"Sitting in the parking lot of the Tennessee Mental Health Center. Doing surveillance on Bill Lance. Why, what's up?"

"Anything happening there?"

"Not a thing. Man goes to work and goes home. Seems to be pretty much a loner."

"Any news on the man at the mission named Cotton?" Lou asked.

"Not really. He's been working there around three years. Had a run of bad luck. He's living with his son on Watkins Street over by the old Sears building. No arrests. Not even a traffic ticket. Seems like a decent enough guy."

"What about our mystery man?"

"You won't believe this one. The car was a rental, and they had his name as Rocky Balboa. Nothing matched up. Address, phone, and ID were all fakes. Couldn't follow any of the paperwork. I need to do some more work on him."

"Okay. I'm going over to where Gary West was shot. I need to check out the area myself. Can you meet me there? We need to talk," Lou said.

"Sure. Nothing going on here."

"The report said he was in the Pier Restaurant parking lot on Wagner Place, right off Beale. I'm heading that way now."

"See you in a bit," Sue said.

Pulling into the parking lot, Lou noticed several orange traffic cones blocking three spaces. The lunchtime crowd had thinned out, and only a few cars remained. As he walked around the restricted area, he scanned the asphalt. The only remains were a few small pieces of broken glass and several oil spots. Crouching down, Lou watched as the wind bounced fragments of trash along the front edge of the asphalt and collected them in a corner next to a concrete wall. Approaching the wall, a legal-size colored flier concealed a handful of trash. Slowly removing the advertisement revealed a collage of paper products. Sitting on top was a Big Red gum wrapper, untouched by the elements. Lou's stomach knotted up immediately. He used his handkerchief to pick up the wrapper and carefully folded it into the cotton cloth.

"You find anything?"

Startled by the sound of Sue's voice, Lou's face turned red from embarrassment. After pretending to wipe his face with the handkerchief, he placed it back in his pocket. "No, nothing. Looks like the CSU cleaned out the place. You look nice."

Sue was wearing a white blouse and a pair of black slacks. Her hair was pulled back in a tight bun.

"Thanks. What are you doing over here?" Sue asked.

"Just took a walk while I was waiting for you."

Sue looked closely at Lou's face and questioned the scratched and bruised area under his eye. "What happened to your face?"

"Fell out of bed. Hit my face on the nightstand."

Sue nodded, but he could tell she didn't believe him. Lou stared at Sue, not sure how to start. "Let's take a walk," he said.

The handkerchief in Lou's back pocket felt like a rock next to his body. He wiped his hands against his shirt several times but couldn't seem to remove the clammy feeling. They turned left on Beale Street, dodged the traffic on Riverside Drive, and walked a short distance to Tom Lee Park. They sat down on a park bench off the pedestrian walkway, facing the Mississippi River. A small tugboat pushed a barge of oil drums from President's Island to a Wolf River dock. The *Memphis Queen* floated motionless inside the wave protection of Mud Island. Lou sat in silence, wringing his hands.

"So, what's up?" asked Sue.

"I've been having some bad dreams. Not really dreams, because I seem to be awake. Visions maybe. Visions that scare me."

Sue looked concerned. She leaned toward him, clasping her hands in her lap. "I'm listening, Lou. Tell me what's going on. I want to know."

"You have any gum?" Lou asked, looking straight ahead at the river.

"Sure. Here you go." Sue offered him a pack of Big Red. Two pieces remained.

Trying not to be obvious, Lou pulled the gum out by the foil wrapper. Only touching a small edge, he slid the gum out and carefully placed the wrapper in his shirt pocket. He immediately felt sick to his stomach. He tore off half a stick and placed the other half in his pants pocket.

Hesitating because of the possible implications of his confession, Lou lowered his head. He took a deep breath. His voice cracked as he began to speak. "I've been seeing ghosts. Not ghosts like you think of ghosts, but ghosts that look like real people—with one exception."

"And that exception is?" inquired Sue.

"Their faces are empty. They have no eyes. They stare at me like they have eyes, but they don't. They haunt me at night and in my dreams. They want something. They want me to do something or find something. I can't get away from that stare. I feel like I'm going crazy."

"Lou, you're not going crazy. You're under a lot of pressure. The mind does funny things when it can't find its way. I have to ask you this because it relates to what is happening. Are you still drinking? You seem to have a—"

"That has nothing to do with it!" Lou snapped at her. "I'm telling you, what is happening to me has nothing to do with that! Can't you just believe what I'm telling you?"

"You asked me here to talk with you. At least I think you did. Don't cut me off when I'm asking you about what's happening."

Lou settled back on the bench and tried to start again.

"Okay. Yes, I still drink, but what I see is not related. I have the visions if I'm drinking or not. One of them involves you."

"What about me?" Sue asked.

"You were standing between two ghosts, and I see you getting shot. Your face goes empty. Like theirs."

"Where was I when this happened?"

"You were in one of the alleys in Cotton Row. It was awful. There was nothing I could do to stop it. It was so real."

"Do you know which alley it was?"

"Yes," Lou replied.

"Can you take me there?"

"Please, don't ask me to do that," Lou pleaded. "I can't do that! I won't!"

Lou wiped the sweat from his face. His heart began to race. His hands trembled. Hiding his face in his hands, he repeated his plea. "Don't ask me to do that."

Sue placed her hands on Lou's wrists, gently pulling his hands away from his face. "Lou, look at me," she said. "Just take me to the alley. I'll be with you. They can't hurt you. They can't hurt me. You have to take this step. Do you want these visions to haunt you all your life?"

Lou shook his head but didn't answer. "There's something else."

"What?"

"I saw myself die too. I saw a bullet enter my head. It was like I was watching it happen. I see visions of death all around me. Sometimes, I'm getting pulled into this hole, and I can't get out. They won't let me out. I can see them standing above me, looking down with their empty faces. Then, one of them drops a shovel of dirt on me. Then another. And another. But most of the time, it's just me standing in the alley. Watching you get shot and a bullet blowing my head apart. I won't take you down there. I can't."

Lou lowered his head. A tear fell on his pants leg and disappeared within seconds, soaking into the fabric.

"Okay, Lou. I understand. Let me talk to the captain and get you scheduled for some help."

"You can't do that. You can't tell anyone. You have to promise me that you won't tell anyone. I need another week. If I can't get my head on straight in another week, I'll go to the captain. I've got a few more days to put my arms around this case. They're trying to tell me something. Maybe it's that I'm going to die. Maybe that is the message. But I won't let them take you with me."

"Lou, they're not going to take either of us. Nobody is going to die. I'll always be here."

"Will you give me another week? I promise I'll tell the captain."

"Yes, I'll do that."

"Could you leave me alone for now? I need to sit here for a few minutes."

"Sure." Sue touched his face and smiled. "Call me if you need to talk again."

Lou nodded and forced a smile. He waited until Sue disappeared from sight. Taking the handkerchief out of his back pocket, he unfolded the cotton cloth. As he placed the wrapper from his shirt pocket next to the one he retrieved from the parking lot, he noted that the red batch color of the two wrappers looked identical. He knew what he should do. Protocol was to take the samples into the lab for color matching and fingerprints. Picking up both wrappers, he tore them into tiny pieces and sprinkled them on the grass.

CHAPTER 11

Return of the Soothsayer

LOU LEFT TOM LEE Park and headed back to the Beale Street District. His mind was flooded with events and pictures. As he crossed Front Street, he stopped for a minute, cleared his mind, and looked down Cotton Row. He felt a cold shiver run through his body. Lou knew that Sue was right, and what he must do. He would have to face his demons and return to this place that was consuming him. Continuing toward his destination, Lou entered the brick streets of the Beale Street District. It was early evening, and crowds were appearing from around every corner. The smell of food cooking and the blues filled the heavy air.

Walking along Beale Street, Lou stopped at Third Street. He spotted Matt sitting on a bench in the W. C. Handy Park. Music was playing over the speakers on each corner of the park. The marker at the park's entrance read, "William Christopher Handy, best known as W. C. Handy, was born November 16, 1873, in Florence, Alabama. Known as the Father of the Blues."

Lou took a seat on the other end of the bench from Matt. Looking straight ahead, he addressed Matt in a very low voice.

"Captain Smitters told me who you are. My name is Lou Cros. I'm an investigator for the Memphis Police Department."

"I know who you are," Matt said, nervously glancing around him, alert for anything that didn't belong.

"Got somewhere we can talk?" Lou asked.

"I'll meet you on the second level of the parking garage across the alley from the Rendezvous. I'll be by the back stairs."

"See you there in ten," Lou said.

Separating, the two men left in different directions. Circling around the Peabody Hotel, Lou entered the alley across the street. As he passed the Rendezvous, he found a break in the chain-link fence and ducked into the parking garage. After walking up the rancid-smelling concrete stairwell, Lou pushed open the heavy door. Matt was standing in the shadow of a concrete-block pilaster.

"Captain said I wasn't to have any contact with anyone but him. This meeting never happened," stated Matt.

"You can't just cut me out! I have more information on this case than anyone," snapped Lou.

"Like I said, this meeting never happened."

"Are you staying at the mission?" Lou asked.

"Been there a couple of days."

"So, what can you tell me?"

"Not much. Janitor named Cotton has a good relationship with most of the people there. He seems to be trusted. Wouldn't tell me much. He's being pretty defensive. He knows Ted and has contact with him. I followed him to a building on Front Street. I saw Ted, but he gave me the slip."

"Gave you the slip? What does that mean?"

"Just what I said. He got away before I could get next to him."

"That's just great! Now you've screwed it up for the rest of us! Are you that incompetent, or is it just this time?"

"This meeting is over. If you contact me again, I'll call the captain," Matt said, obviously angry with Lou.

"I don't like threats." Lou pushed Matt backward a few steps.

"You better back off, or I'll add to those scars on your face, old man!"

Lou started to move in again, but then he hesitated.

Matt gave Lou a short push back. "If you were doing your job, they wouldn't have called me in! And don't ever touch me again! Do you understand?"

"Yeah, I understand! You're incompetent all the time," Lou said.

Matt stared at Lou for a few seconds, as if deciding whether to punch him out or not, and then he quickly left through the stairwell. "I'm out of here," he said under his breath.

Lou watched as Matt left. Slamming an open hand on the pilaster, Lou regretted that his temper might have kept him from getting the information he needed to find Ted.

Back on Beale Street, Jack and Dave were walking their beat and watching the growing evening crowds. Other than the usual boasting loudmouths and some friendly shoving, everything seemed under control.

"There's Lou," Dave said. "Wonder what he's doing here again tonight?"

Jack looked over the crowd and saw Lou at the far end of the strip. "Probably looking for a drink."

"Come on, Jack. Give the guy a break. He's been under a lot of pressure."

"We're all under a lot of pressure. I'm not judging him. I just call it as I see it."

Changing the subject, Dave quickly pulled Jack's mind away from Lou. "I need a Coke. How about you?"

"No, I'm good."

Dave stopped at the next open service window and ordered a Coke and a small basket of fries. "Need to get me a little energy," he joked.

Jack's grin was wiped away as he spotted the preacher man at the Third Street corner. "Preacher's back," he said.

The gangly body of the soothsayer was dressed in black jeans and a white shirt. The long sleeves were rolled up halfway on his arms. His stringy hair was draped down over his beard on either side. He was carrying a worn leather-bound Bible in one hand. Holding the Bible high in the air, he cried out to the crowd.

"Shelter us against the tumult of evildoers, who sharpen their teeth like swords and aim like arrows their bitter words, shooting from ambush at the innocent man. Our enemy assaults us and brings down evil upon us. This enemy is a deceiver. He devises a wicked scheme and slowly penetrates into an unguarded heart. Repent of your sins. Cast out the beast that enslaves you. Evil walks among us. I can feel its presence."

"I'm going to walk down there," started Jack. "It'll help with crowd control."

"I'll be there in a minute," replied Dave, waiting for his order.

"This beast came out of the sea," continued the soothsayer. "He has ten horns and seven heads. One of the heads has a mark of a sword but still lives. A number will mark his followers. They will bear the number of the evil one: 666."

As Jack walked up, some of the crowd moved on. A young man raised his cup of beer as if making a toast. "Amen, preacher," he yelled out. "I have him here in this cup." Laughing, he tipped the cup and drank the remains. The other young men around him all raised their cups and followed suit.

"The faint of mind are easily deceived!" the preacher shouted back. "Be on guard, for we know not the day or the hour of judgment! Repent your sins!"

"I think the preacher just called you stupid!" someone in the crowd shouted to the man who had tipped his cup.

Jack stepped between the two potential combatants. "Okay, guys, move along. Show's over."

As Dave walked up, the group moved on, laughing and pushing each other along. The soothsayer continued his preaching. "One walks among us with the cloak of a lamb! I feel his presence! Don't be deceived! He has been loosed after a thousand years! His fruit is poisoned, and his soul is black! Death is his sting, and damnation is his path!"

Jack's attention was drawn to the north end of Beale. Another skirmish was taking place in the street between two men. Tempers were flaring, and fingers were beginning to point.

"What the heck is this?" questioned Jack. "Is it a full moon or what?"

Seeing Dave down the street, Jack motioned for him. Jack had to grin as he watched Dave sigh and dump his french fries and Coke into a trash barrel. Just as they reached the trouble spot, one of the men backed off. Jack walked between them to break the stare-down. The two walked away.

"Nicely done." Jack recognized Lou's voice. "Glad you two came along. I wasn't looking forward to sticking my nose in there."

Jack nodded but gave no response.

"Come on, Jack. You can't still be mad."

"No, I'm not mad. Just have a lot on my mind. I don't need to be dealing with your problems too."

"Come on, man. I said I was sorry. Don't you love me anymore?" teased Lou.

Jack cracked a smile. "I still love you, man."

"Now, Dave, if you would leave us alone, we have some making up to do." Lou placed his arm around Jack's shoulder and smiled.

"All right, you two. Break it up," said Dave, smiling back at Lou.

The ringing of Lou's cell phone broke the convivial moment. Glancing at the caller ID, he held it up for Jack to see. It was from Captain Smitters.

"Hello?" Lou put his index finger to his lips as a message to Jack and Dave.

"Yes, sir." Lou got a worried look on his face. "I'm on Beale Street with officers Jack Mills and Dave Drake. Yes, sir. Jack is right here. Yes, sir." Lou handed the phone to Jack. "He wants to speak to you."

"Jack Mills. Yes, sir. Yes, sir, I understand." Handing the phone back to Lou, he gave Dave a questioning look.

"What's up, Captain?" Lou asked.

"Lou, I have a problem," stated Captain Smitters. "I have an eyewitness who said you were at Gary West's apartment before his murder. Were you there?"

"I may have been over that way," Lou answered.

"Cut the crap! Were you there?"

"Yes, I believe I did stop by."

"I find nothing in your report about this. Why do I not have a report that you visited a man's apartment before he was murdered?"

"I was going to tell you about it. I was just following up on something else. I planned on briefing you on it as soon as I was able to put something together."

"Not good enough, Lou. An eyewitness puts you in contact with the victim. As of right now, you're being suspended from duty until an IAD investigation is complete. You need to give Officer Mills your badge and gun, and I want you here at 9:00 AM to make a statement. IAD wants to talk with you. You don't mess with the Internal Affairs Department, Lou. Don't even think about it. You are officially off this case. Do you understand me?"

"Yes, sir. I understand. May I ask who is this eyewitness?"

"Not at this time. You be here in the morning. Now, give Officer Mills the phone back."

Totally frustrated, Lou listened to Jack's one-sided conversation.

"What is going on?" questioned Dave.

Jack closed Lou's phone and handed it back to him. Turning to Dave, Jack said, "It seems that Lou had prior contact with Gary West that wasn't reported. Then West shows up dead. Not real smart on your part, Lou, because IAD is going to think you covered up the connection between you and the victim. Sorry, Lou, but I need your badge and gun."

"This is not right!" Lou's voice began to elevate. Several people on the street turned to see what was happening. "They can't take me off this case! I'm being set up!"

"Lou, don't push on this until you've talked with IAD and the captain," Jack said. "You need to pull yourself together and present your case. You know the protocol."

Lou's face turned red with anger. "I can't believe the captain had me tailed!"

"You don't know that," Jack said. "It may have come from the Feds. It sounds like the case has been turned over to them." Jack paused a minute to let Lou calm down. "Lou, I need your badge and gun," he said in a gentle voice.

Lou took out his badge and handed it over. "I don't carry my gun on me. It's in the car."

"Dave, Lou and I are going to take a walk to his car. If you don't mind, just watch the street for a few minutes until I get back."

"Sure, Jack. I can do that."

As Lou turned to walk with Jack, he noticed a familiar face in the crowd. "Wait a minute, Jack. I think I see someone."

A side view of Rocky's face disappeared among a group of tourists.

"Who is it?" asked Jack.

"Nobody. Just thought I saw someone. It's nobody."

"You sure?"

"Yeah, it's nobody."

Jack and Lou walked in silence. Jack broke the awkwardness. "Talk to me, Lou. What's going on?"

"I think I'm being set up. Captain said he has an eyewitness that saw me at West's apartment. Someone must have tailed me there. All this is insane."

"What can you tell me about West?"

"It wasn't a big deal. I wanted to know if he saw anything the night of one of the shootings. He was with a bunch of guys that night, and he saw someone follow the homeless man out of the district. I pushed him a little. I think he knew more than he was saying."

"So, you don't think it was a drug deal gone bad?"

"No. No, I don't."

When the two arrived at the car in the Pier Restaurant parking lot, Lou handed his gun to Jack.

"I know that telling you to back off this case will be a waste of breath, but I'm saying it for the record. Now, off the record, you need to keep me posted on any information you come up with. Starting now," Jack said. "Who did you see back in the district?"

"Nobody, Jack. I swear. It was nobody."

Jack nodded, but he obviously didn't believe Lou.

"You can help me, Jack," Lou said. "I need you to try to find out who this eyewitness is. This person is involved. I think I was getting too close. I'm being taken out on purpose."

"I'll see what I can do. That also makes you a possible victim. Watch your back."

"I will, Jack. Thanks."

Jack walked back into the Beale Street District and found Dave. Strolling down Beale, Jack told him all he knew about West and the eyewitness. The soothsayer remained on the curb, shouting at the patrons of the restaurants. Pointing his finger over the crowd, he made eye contact with Jack and Dave.

"Don't be deceived!" he shouted. "He wears the cloak of a lamb, and death is his sting!"

CHAPTER 12

The Encounter

LOU WAITED OUTSIDE CAPTAIN Smitters's office, staring into his empty coffee cup. The clock on the wall read straight up 9:00 AM. The door was closed, and he heard muffled conversation inside. Walking to the coffee machine, he passed by the door. The talking and banging of computer keyboards in the general office made it impossible to clearly hear anything behind the closed door. Pouring half a cup of coffee, he glanced around the office. Watchful eyes darted back to their workstations. Lou looked into a small mirror hanging on the wall. He looked like he had been on an all-night drunk. Bloodshot eyes and an unshaven face indicated that he had had a restless night. Lou's attention was moved to the sound of the captain's turning doorknob. Jack and Dave exited the open door. Looking over at Lou, Jack's face was blank, impossible to read.

"Come on in, Lou, and have a seat," Captain Smitters said.

As Lou passed by Captain Smitters, the captain leaned close to Lou's ear and whispered to him, "You look like hell! Tuck in your shirt!"

After responding to Captain Smitters's request, Lou took a seat along the front wall.

"Lou, this is Captain David Rash with Internal Affairs. They're aware of your current suspension pending an IAD investigation. This interview is being recorded." Captain Smitters began reading a document handed to him by the

Captain Rash. "Any information gathered today will be held in confidence with the mayor's office and cannot be used in any criminal proceedings. Any criminal proceedings that may or may not occur in the future will constitute a separate investigation. Do you understand these proceedings?"

"Yes," Lou confirmed.

Handing the document back over to Captain Rash, Captain Smitters turned the meeting over to him. The first few minutes of the interview were taken up with verifying Lou's personal information. Flipping sheets on a notepad, Captain Rash started discussing the incident in question.

"Detective Cros, I have taken statements from Officers Jack Mills and Dave Drake. Do you know both of these officers?"

"Yes, I know them," Lou replied.

"I understand from their statement that you met them the other night in the Beale Street District outside the Hard Rock Café. At that time, you told them about a meeting you had with Mr. Gary West at his apartment. Is that true?"

"Maybe. I don't remember."

"In Officer Dave Drake's statement, he indicated that you admitted to having a physical altercation with Mr. West that left a knot below your eye. He quotes you as saying, 'He decided to try to take me out. His mistake.' Is that accurate?"

"Yes."

"Later that same day, Mr. West was seen at B.B. King's and the Rum Boogie Café. You were also seen in the same area. The issue here, Detective Cros, is that there was no report of your meeting or of any physical altercation between you and Mr. West that may have transpired. So, it seems that you were the last one to have knowledge of Mr. West's whereabouts before his murder later that night. Do you understand the gravity of this incident?"

"Yes."

"Can you tell us why there was no information reported relating to Mr. West?" Captain Rash asked.

"No, I just didn't have enough time to get it all done," Lou said.

"When you say you didn't have enough time, what are you referring to?"

"The report! I didn't do one lousy report! That doesn't mean I killed the slug!" Lou felt his anger growing and took a deep breath to calm down.

"Detective Cros, your fingerprints and one of your business cards were in Mr. West's apartment. Also in the apartment were illegal guns and drugs. Are you telling us that this information was not reported because you didn't deem your meeting important?"

"Yes, it wasn't a big deal!" Lou paused a minute. "It was just a follow-up."

"When you say follow-up, you're referring to the prior investigation involving Mr. West at the Greyhound Bus Terminal, where another murder took place?"

"When you say it like that, it sounds more important than it was," Lou replied.

"So, let me recap your statement. You were doing a follow-up visit with Mr. Gary West for a murder investigation. During this follow-up, you had a physical altercation with Mr. West. That night, you and he were seen in the Beale Street District. Later, Mr. West shows up dead. Your statement is that a report wasn't made because you didn't think this information was important. Is that your statement?"

Lou looked over at Captain Smitters. The captain leaned back in his chair but offered no empathy or support. "Yes, that's right."

"Is there anything else you would like to add?"

Lou's mind drifted off. How could he have been so reckless? He was losing his edge. He felt like he had failed the captain, and like he had failed himself.

"Detective Cros?"

Lou's attention was drawn back to the meeting.

"Is there anything else you would like to add?"

"No, nothing," Lou said.

"Thank you, Detective Cros. Captain Smitters will be in touch with you."

Lou walked through the office, heading to his car. He felt like all eyes were watching him. Once in his car, he sat in silence. The questioning had triggered Lou's memory, a very particular memory.

He was sitting at a table in an interrogation room. Across from him was a drug dealer. The dealer was a white male in his early thirties. His head was shaved. He was wearing an earring in his right ear. His open-collar Hawaiian shirt was spotted with blood. He had a black Fu Manchu mustache that ended at his chin. Two front gold teeth, surrounded by stark white ceramic caps, reflected in the overhead light. Lou remembered the feeling of hate building up inside him. How badly he wanted to stick his gun in the dealer's grinning face and end this man's wretched life. Lou remembered what it felt like being pulled off the drug dealer by two officers when he exploded across the table and pounded the man's face. That was his first suspension, which lasted only a month. Another inmate delivered the drug dealer's sentence while he was awaiting trial.

Lou stared out from the concrete steps of the Cossitt Library on Front Street. It was early afternoon. Across the street and to the right of his vantage point was Cotton Row. He recalled the old downtown, when the library steps were filled with students reading or taking a break from their research. Mothers and children carried books, excited about their next adventure. Cotton merchants and porters walked the street, shaking hands and exchanging life stories. Bales of cotton wrapped in brown canvas lined the shops on Cotton Row. Children chased the tiny clouds of cotton fibers floating through the air like dandelion seeds. Women carried shopping bags of merchandise from Goldsmith's, the John Gerber Company, Lowenstein's, Oak Hall, S. H. Kress, and Julius Lewis retailers. But in the 1960s, a mass exodus to the growing suburban areas of Memphis began, leaving behind a downtown struggling for a new identity.

Massive rain clouds dropped low in the sky and formed a ghostly gray line above the lighter-colored horizon. The smell of dust-laden moisture alerted the senses of an oncoming storm. As the darkening sky enveloped the city, automatic streetlights flickered on. A river tugboat whistle sounded, as the vessel made its way upriver. A mixture of vegetation and paper trash danced through the street, seeking shelter from the rising wind.

In his depressed state, Lou's mind plunged into the darkness that surrounded him. He felt the weight of failure and rejection. He questioned his existence and what purpose he had served. Maybe he shouldn't have come back to the force. His instincts weren't as sharp as they had been before. He had trouble focusing. He was screwing up big-time. Sue was right. He was acting like a rookie.

Looking down the street, Lou's hands trembled as he viewed the boarded-up buildings along Cotton Row. A figure walked down the sidewalk, stopping occasionally at the padlocked doors. In spite of the darkening sky and the distance, he could tell it was a woman about the same size and build of Sue. As she passed one of the alleyways, Lou saw a tall silhouette emerge from within. Jumping to his feet, he screamed, "No!"

The sound of Lou's voice was drowned out in the swirling winds. Racing toward the woman, he screamed again, "Get away from her!"

The black figure dropped back into the alley. The woman stopped in her tracks and looked up at the shouting man. From his current distance, Lou could see the woman's stringy white hair hanging down a skeletal face. The eye sockets were void of any tissue. He froze. Sweat flooded his skin.

"What do you want? Why do you torture me?" he screamed.

The woman quickly turned and disappeared in the alleyway. Unable to control his shaking body, Lou slowly walked to the opening of the alleyway. The building walls on both sides of the alley seemed to close in and shut out the remaining light. A flash of lightning confirmed that this was the same alley where he'd had his death premonition. The woman stepped out of the building wall.

"What do you want from me?" Lou screamed.

Raising her finger, she pointed at the third floor of the building. Lou grabbed his pounding head. "Leave me alone! I won't go!" Overcome by the pain in his head, Lou struggled to keep his consciousness. Another bolt of lightning flashed a hideous view of another world. The woman's ghostly face morphed from the skeletal remains to Sue and then morphed back again. "You can't have her!" he screamed. "Leave her alone! I'll never let her go!"

Turning her head and looking up at the third floor, the woman pointed again. Lights blinked inside the third-floor windows. Contorted faces pressed their cheeks against the broken glass. Skeletal hands stretched out through the jagged holes, as the spiny fingers opened and closed, beckoning Lou inside. As if under the woman's spell, he unwillingly took a step forward. Just as he was about to take another step, he heard a car pull up next to the curb. The apparitions disappeared back into the darkness.

"Lou, is that you?"

Lou turned around and reached out for help, struggling to keep his balance. He felt faint. Dave jumped out of the patrol car and grabbed Lou by the arm. Lou's body immediately collapsed. Dragging him to the patrol car, Dave leaned Lou's body against the front fender. Drops of rain began to bounce off the car's hood. Jack jumped from the driver's side and helped Dave place Lou in the backseat. "Let's get him to the hospital," Dave said.

As he tried to get out of the car, Lou said, "No, I'm okay." His voice was weak, more like a moan.

"Lou, you need to go to the hospital and get checked out. Your face is white. Something is wrong," Dave said.

"No, I'm not going. Just let me sit here a minute."

"What are you doing over here?" asked Jack.

"I don't know. I was down the street at the library. I thought I saw someone, but it was nobody."

"Lou, you keep seeing a lot of people who turn out to be nobody. You've got to level with us. We can't help if you won't let us in," pushed Jack. "Who did you see?"

"Nobody. It was nobody," repeated Lou.

The rain increased, and Jack and Dave got into the car's front seat. The three men were silent. The sound of the rain whipping the patrol car's chassis dampened the heavy breathing coming from the backseat. Dave was the first to speak. "Lou, I'm sorry about the investigation this morning. I never realized that the report would go that far."

"Forget it, man," Lou said. "You were just doing your job, which is more than I can say for myself. Any information on the eyewitness?"

Jack put the patrol car in drive and eased down Front Street. "No, the records are sealed up in Smitters's office. You sure you don't want us to drop by the hospital?" he asked.

"No, I'm fine. Thanks. If you don't mind, just drop me off at the Peabody Hotel."

"I can do that. By the way, I tried to reach you several times after your meeting. What's going on with your phone?" asked Jack.

"I cut it off. Just didn't feel like talking to anyone," Lou replied.

"Well, do yourself a favor and cut it back on. You never know when you might need it. It also lets us know that you're okay."

"Sure, Jack."

Jack continued. "Lou, you need to stay away from this case. Any involvement will just make it harder on your investigation. That being said, if anything comes up about today, you got caught in the rain, and we just gave you a ride over to the Peabody."

"Thanks, Jack."

The patrol car stopped at the side door of the Peabody Hotel. Still a little uneasy on his feet, Lou said good-bye to Jack and Dave and got out of the car. He walked up to the hotel entrance, pushed the glass door open, and entered the lobby. Hoping that Jack and Dave hadn't seen him stumble, he found the first available chair in the lounge area and plopped down. Checking his watch, Lou was surprised that it was already 3:00 PM. At the bar area, two waitresses were having a discussion and looking over at Lou. He took a quick assessment of himself and understood why. He looked like a bum who came off the street trying to get in out of the rain. He figured they were probably drawing straws, and the loser would have to wait on him. Tucking his shirttail in and running his fingers through his hair, he tried to look more presentable. It didn't help. Another minute passed before one of them approached.

"May I help you with something?" the waitress asked.

"Just a Coke," replied Lou.

"That will be three dollars." The young lady stood in place.

Lou looked up and got the message. "I don't always look this way." Lou handed her a five-dollar bill. "Keep the change."

Using her thumb and index finger, she pinched the money out of his trembling hand.

"And bring me a menu when you come back. I may want to stay here a while. I hear you specialize in duck." Lou was jabbing back at the young waitress. He knew that the Peabody Hotel was known for its parade of ducks that ride the elevator down from their rooftop home twice a day.

The waitress quickly returned with a Coke and a menu. She placed the items on the side table next to Lou and scurried away.

Lou's trembling hand attempted to pick up the Coke with little success. Looking toward the bar, his waitress turned away, as if she hadn't noticed. His body ached, and his breathing was labored. There was some movement inside the atrium shops. Lou focused in on Lansky Brothers Clothier. He got a snippet glance of Rocky standing behind a rack of Elvis Presley limited-edition shirts. As soon as Lou made eye contact, Rocky moved back into the shop and out of sight. Jumping up from his chair, Lou lost his balance. As he fell backward into his chair, he knocked his drink onto the floor. Customers looked up. Lou's waitress turned her back, pretending she hadn't seen what had happened. The other waitress grinned and turned away. The lobby started to spin out of control. He grabbed his head, closed his eyes, and counted to ten. Reassuring himself that all was back to normal, he pushed himself up from the chair and staggered to Lansky's inside glass storefront. Casing the shop, he saw that Rocky had vanished.

CHAPTER 13

Rocky

UNABLE TO LOCATE GLITTER at the Burger King, Lou headed for the only other person who would know of Rocky's whereabouts. He was sure this man was tailing him. Entering John's Pawnshop, he found Glitter's brother standing behind the counter.

"I need to find Glitter. Do you know where he is?"

Lifting up the hinged counter section, John Henry motioned with his head. "He's in the back." Stepping in front of Lou, he blocked his entry. "No weapons allowed."

Holding his arms up, Lou waited for a pat down just as he heard Glitter's voice coming from the back room.

"Is that Lou Cros I hear out there? Let the man through," Glitter said.

John Henry stepped aside. Pulling back a dark brown hanging curtain, Lou entered the back room. The room was a cluttered office area with a stained oak desk, complete with a phone and computer. In the middle of the floor was a round wooden table with six chairs. Glitter was sitting at the table with two other men. A bottle of Jack Daniels whiskey and four glasses were spaced around the table. Folders and cash receipts were spread about. Lou noticed a four-section wall monitor that covered all areas of the front shop.

"Nice place you have here," said Lou.

"Nice place!" Glitter said, laughing at Lou's comment. "Sit down a minute and take a load off." Staring at Lou's unshaven and bruised face, Glitter took a sip of his whiskey. "You look like hell." Looking over to the man on his right, he motioned with the glass in hand. "Get the man a clean glass and turn that music down."

Lou waved off the offer. The music playing in the background was a song Lou recognized as "That Old Black Magic," a recording by Louis Prima and Keely Smith.

"Now, what can I do for you?" asked Glitter.

"I've been suspended from the force."

"Tell me something I don't know," said Glitter, grinning.

Looking around the table, Lou took in the new faces. Next to Glitter, on his right, was a hulk of a man. Judging from his height in the chair, Lou pegged him at a whopping six-four, and with a weight topping three hundred pounds. He was black and had a shaved head. A jagged scar ran over his right eyebrow. His nose sat crooked on his face. Lou guessed his age to be around thirty. He was wearing a dark gray round-neck T-shirt. His calloused knuckles jutted from his massive hands like white quarters. Next to him was a smaller man, also black, who was about the same age or maybe a little younger. He had short hair and a small mustache. His features were similar to John Henry's.

"Are you going to introduce me to your friends?" asked Lou.

"My, my! Where are my manners?" joked Glitter. "Next to me is Mike. He's my new financial assistant. Next to him is my little brother. We call him Little G. Man's got a great business mind. Graduated from the University of Memphis at the head of his class. Watches our books for us. You can talk in front of them."

"I need your help. That guy Rocky you were with the other day? He's following me. I need to find out who he is and why he's on my tail."

"I've already had him checked out. Tell him, Little G," Glitter said.

Little G took over for Glitter. "His cell phone is a Detroit number. He's got a block on it. Can't look it up. All incoming calls are rerouted from Michigan to a message box in another state. A computer picks it up there and passes it to an overseas satellite that sends it back here. Pretty sophisticated technology."

"Isn't he impressive?" declared Glitter, making a toast to Little G.

"He looks like an army brat," continued Little G. "But I can't get his real name. He's staying at the Dixie Hotel on South Third Street. One of those places you can pay by the day or by the week. Pays cash for everything. His car is registered in Detroit to a Rocky Balboa. You know, like Sylvester Stallone in the *Rocky* movies? Paid cash for it too. Address on the registration turns out to be the YMCA. He's also been asking questions on the street about Glitter. Sounds like a cop, doesn't he? You sure he's not one of yours?"

"Yeah, I got a beeline on an undercover agent working the case. He's not the guy. No way they would have two on the same case. Too much conflict."

Glitter nodded and said, "Then the other option is that he's working for the Detroit boys, maybe looking to expand down South. I've asked some of my contacts in Detroit to see what they can find out. So far, nobody seems to know anything about this guy. He's a real mystery."

Lou leaned forward to make a point. "How about we watch each of our backs for the other guy. It sounds to me like this guy is becoming a thorn in your side. Maybe between the two of us we can send Mr. Rocky Balboa back to Detroit."

Glitter took another sip of his Jack Daniels. "Are you asking me to partner up with a cop?"

"Suspended cop," Lou corrected.

Glitter looked over at Little G, who gave a nod.

"What if we need to use a little muscle?" asked Glitter.

"That's your call," Lou said. "I'm off the force right now. I can look the other way as long as Mr. Balboa doesn't turn up dead. Maybe you haven't heard? I'm real bad with paperwork."

"So, Mr. Detective, how do we go about finding this guy?" Glitter asked.

"We don't need to find him. He'll find us. He's been hanging around the Beale Street District. I saw him in the area this afternoon before he disappeared. My best bet is that he's still there. All I have to do is reappear."

"So, you're kind of like the bait? I like that," Glitter said. Turning to his right, he addressed Mike. "You have any problems?"

Mike shook his head and said, "None."

"I need a small microphone to put on Mike," Lou said. "Something that has an earplug that I can listen in on. If Rocky pulls a weapon, I need to know when to jump in."

Glitter turned to his younger brother. "You still got that little spy pen? It was in the front cabinet."

"Yeah, I can put some new batteries in it, and it will be ready to go."

Glitter wrote a number on a piece of paper and slid the paper over in front of Lou. "That's our phone number. Memorize it. I don't want it showing up on your body somewhere," Glitter joked. Holding up his glass, Glitter gave Lou a toast. "Welcome, partner."

The lunch crowd on Beale Street was thinning out. The rain had stopped, leaving behind walls of humid air and streaks of sunshine. Small puddles of water filled the voids of the uneven brick pavement. Curling streams of water trickled along the concrete curb and fell between the metal bars of the sewer grates.

Lou sat at a corner table outside the Hard Rock Café. He pushed away an untouched hamburger, as the smell of cooked meat nauseated him. From there, he had a good view of the street. Mike sat inside Silky O'Sullivan's next to the glass wall and sipped a beer. Within the hour, Rocky appeared. Darting in and out of open doors, he found his perch inside B.B. King's. Lou stood up and dropped ten dollars on the table. Walking away from the district, he signaled Mike about the contact.

Mike left Silky O'Sullivan's and cut through a side street over to Union Avenue, working his way to a parking garage built on the demolished site of the Lowe's Palace Theatre. Mike slipped behind a parked van and waited. Lou entered the parking garage's first level and proceeded to his car. Within minutes, Rocky presented himself in the area. Walking leisurely down Union Avenue, he stopped at an alcove and leaned against the inside wall. Watching from inside the garage, Lou watched Mike exit out the back and circle around to Rocky's blind side. Moving over to the concrete retaining wall, Lou saw Mike was in position. Rocky stepped out of the alcove. Surprised at seeing Mike in his path, Rocky took a step back and checked the street for other surprises.

Lou moved closer, so that the sound in the earpiece would be clearer.

"Glitter wants to see you," Mike said.

"I don't think so. If Glitter wanted to see me, he would have left me a message," Rocky said.

"The word on the street is that you've been asking too many questions," Mike continued.

"I don't know what you're talking about." Rocky took a step to the outside, attempting to pass. Mike blocked his move. Rocky took another step back and stared into Mike's eyes. It took Rocky less than a second to deliver a roundhouse kick to the side of Mike's head. The blow knocked Mike off balance, as he struggled to stay on his feet. Rocky drew his fist back in karate-style and delivered a quick set of combination punches to Mike's torso. Falling backward, Mike caught himself against the brick wall of the building. Pushing off the wall, Mike grabbed Rocky in a bear hug and lifted him off his feet. Letting out a huge groan, Mike applied rib-crushing pressure.

Unable to move his arms, Rocky rammed his forehead into Mike's face, splintering his nose. Mike fell back from the pain and force of the head butt and released his hold. Wiping the blood from his nose, he charged in. Rocky jumped in the air and tried to deliver a straight kick to Mike's throat. Mike's huge hand grabbed the foot in midair and twisted. Rocky fell to the sidewalk, ripping open his shoulder as the force of his body dragged against the concrete. As Mike leaned over, Rocky swift-kicked him in the face, sending him back against the wall.

By this time, Lou decided he needed to step in before a weapon appeared. Lou rushed out from behind the car, yelling at both men. Several people in cars had passed and had beeped the horn in an attempt to stop the fight. A police car siren grew louder. Rocky struggled to his feet, limped to an alleyway, and disappeared. Just as Lou reached Mike, Jack and Dave pulled up.

"Where the hell have you guys been?" shouted Lou. "I called you twenty minutes ago!"

"Lou, you just called," replied Jack. "What's going on?"

Mike wiped the blood from below his nose.

"White dude tried to rob me," Mike said.

"That's true," Lou said. "I saw the whole thing."

"Give me a break. You're telling me a white guy jumped *this* man in broad daylight on Union Avenue?" Jack asked.

"That's right," Lou said. "The guy was crazy. I think I know him. Yes, I know I've seen him before. His name is Rocky Balboa. He's staying at the Dixie Hotel on South Third Street. You guys need to check him out."

"Rocky Balboa," laughed Jack. "Come on, Lou, don't waste the precinct's time on a wild-goose chase."

"I'm telling you, Jack. This guy is for real."

"Okay, Lou. Hold on. Did he have a weapon?"

"You know, I couldn't really tell. I mean it all happened so fast," Lou replied.

"How about you?" Jack asked, turning to question Mike. "I mean it happened so fast, you probably couldn't tell, either, could you?"

"Ah, no. I guess not," Mike said.

"Now, Jack. I know that Captain Smitters would be very disappointed if he found out that there was a possible armed robbery that took place and nobody checked it out. Wouldn't you say so?" Lou asked.

"Okay, Lou. You've made your point. Dave, take some information from this gentleman while I have a talk with Lou."

Leaving Dave to take Mike's statement, Jack grabbed Lou by the arm and walked him far enough away from Dave and Mike to be out of earshot. "What are you doing, Lou? This whole thing is a crock. You're going to get fired if you don't stop meddling in this case."

"Jack, this Rocky guy is involved somehow. I can't do my job, so I need you to check him out."

"It would've been a lot simpler if you would've just asked. Why do you want to run up a red flag on your head?"

"Just check this guy out. Please. Do this one thing for me, and I promise I'll leave it alone. Come on, Jack. Help me out. Please, Jack. I need your help."

"Okay, Lou, I'll call this in. But if you're not telling me the truth …"

"It's the truth, Jack. I swear to you."

"It better be," Jack said. "Take care of yourself, Lou."

Lou said he would and headed straight for his car. He figured that Rocky knew the cops would be looking for him. Turning on Third Street, Lou located the Dixie Hotel and parked in an empty lot across the street. A police car was outside the registration office. Two police officers and a black man exited one of the hotel doors. Walking back to the registration office, the two officers shook hands with the day manager and returned to their car. Within a few minutes, the patrol car pulled away. Lou crossed the street and entered the hotel office. The manager was still standing on the customer side of the counter, pouring himself a cup of coffee.

"Excuse me, sir," said Lou. "My name is J. C. Webb. I'm an investigator for the Memphis Police Department." He flashed his empty wallet. "I just got a call from the two officers that left. They asked me to take a look at one more item in Mr. Rocky Balboa's room. I know you're busy, so if you would just loan me the key, I'll do a quick follow-up and leave you alone."

"You're welcome to look. Nothing there. Room 120." The manager handed Lou the key.

"Thank you. I'll be right back."

Lou raced from the office, and a few minutes later, he entered Rocky's room. The room looked like someone was in a hurry to get out. A small TV sat on a desk. The empty drawers were pulled halfway out. The sheets that were on the bed had been removed, exposing a stained mattress. A strong smell of Clorox bleach lingered in the air, indicating that someone had recently wiped the place down. From Lou's experience in forensics, he knew that bleach destroyed DNA, making it impossible to get a positive ID from any DNA testing. He concluded that the sheets were probably taken for the same reason.

Next to the bed was a nightstand with a phone. The receiver was sitting upside down in the cradle and probably hadn't been used. A tattered Memphis phone book and a Gideon's Bible shared a space in the open frame of the stand. Lou noticed that a small piece of one of the pages was crimped in the phone book, forming a thin void between the pages. Opening the book, it took Lou to the yellow pages section of pawnshops. A page was torn out that would have listed John's Pawnshop. Throwing the phone book on the stained mattress, Lou stepped into the bathroom. The odor of Clorox burned his nose. There were no towels, washcloths, or trashcans anywhere in the room. Lou took a last look around and returned to the office. The day manager was sitting in the lobby watching TV.

"Just put the key on the counter," said the manager.

"Thanks for your help. Say, what happened to the sheets and towels?" Lou asked.

"Guy said he spilled ink on them. Gave me a hundred bucks and took them with him."

"Don't you find that odd?"

"Don't ask questions. The man paid for them, so he can have 'em."

"What time did he leave?"

"Right before you guys got here. Paid me for the sheets and left."

"I don't suppose you've seen anyone with him? Maybe a lady friend?"

"I don't look, so I can't tell. I mind my own business, and they mind theirs."

"Thanks again," Lou said. The manager held up his hand in response.

As soon as Lou reached his car, he placed a call to John Henry. On the third ring, he got impatient. "Come on, man! Pick up."

Glitter glanced up at the monitor as John Henry reached for the wall phone in the front of the shop. He was surprised when he saw Rocky burst in the front door. He then watched as John Henry rushed to the hinged countertop and pulled a pistol from under the counter. Before he could level the gun, Rocky slammed through the opening, grabbed John Henry's gun hand, and smashed it against the back wall. As John Henry dropped the gun, Rocky grabbed him by the throat. John Henry gasped for air. Glitter quickly removed a sawed-off pistol-grip shotgun from a desk drawer. Concealing the shotgun under the desk, he placed it in his lap. Rocky forced John Henry into the back room. Sitting behind the desk, Glitter cocked the hammer on the shotgun. The phone on Glitter's desk continued to ring. Pushing John Henry to the desk, Rocky was careful to keep John in front of him.

Rocky took a hard look at Glitter. "Next time you send one of your goons for me, I'm coming after you!" Rocky pushed John Henry half over the desk and picked up the ringing desk phone.

"Yeah?" Rocky held if off his ear so Glitter could hear.

"I think Rocky might be heading your way!" Lou shouted.

"It's for you," said a smiling Rocky, handing the phone to Glitter. "Take it with your right hand."

Sliding his right hand off the shotgun, Glitter took the receiver. After placing the phone to his ear for a few seconds, he returned it to the cradle. "Wrong number."

Rocky pushed off on John Henry, backed out of the room, and left the building.

Chapter 14

Cotton

Pete Johnson looked over the register book at the mission. "Here it is. Just one new patron since you were in here last." Showing the book to Jim Damos, he pointed to the date at the top. "Came in a couple of days ago. Name is Matt. Quiet guy. Stays mostly to himself. He seems to be accepted by the others. He's gotten a few odd jobs, cleaning mostly. Hasn't signed back in today. I saw a few of his things on his bunk. I'm pretty sure he'll be back. Any chance you can stay a while and help serve dinner? I can always use a good hand."

"Sure, Pete. I'll be glad to. If you don't mind, I'll stick my head in the back and speak to Cotton. I like to keep in touch with him. How's he doing?"

"Cotton is a godsend. He's great with people, and he really helps me here."

After a little more small talk, Jim walked down the hall. He found Cotton leaning on a broom in the dormitory room and chatting with some of the patrons. Seeing Jim enter the room, Cotton broke out in a big smile. Jim gave Cotton a hug and patted him on the back.

"Good to see you," Jim said. "You're looking great. How is your work going?"

"This ain't work. This is like retirement," Cotton said, smiling.

"You taking good care of my friends?"

147

"Always, just like you took care of me. I can't thank you enough for all you did. You saved my life."

"You're very welcome. Now it's your turn. Mr. Johnson says you're doing a great job. I'm really proud of you."

"Thanks, Jim." Cotton looked away for a few seconds to hide the buildup of tears in his eyes. "So, did you come by to help out?"

"Yeah, I'm going to stay for a little while. I also wanted to see how everyone here is doing. There's a real concern for their safety." Looking around the room, Jim counted ten people.

"Everyone is a little scared," Cotton said. "The cops are still looking for that murderer, so most of the guys don't go out at night, with the exception of the new guy. He goes by the name of Matt. He's a strange one. He don't seem scared to go out for nothing."

Jim took Cotton by his arm and led him into the back room away from the others. "Tell me about this Matt."

"He came in a couple of days ago. Said he was looking for Ted. Said he was supposed to meet him here. When I spoke with Ted, Ted said he didn't know the guy."

"There're a lot of people looking for Ted. Do you know if he's okay?" asked Jim.

"Ted's good. I don't know why everyone is looking for him. He ain't done anything."

"The police believe he might be able to identify the murderer. He may have some important information."

"Ted says the police are trying to kill him," Cotton said.

"Why would the police want to kill him?"

"I don't know, but that's what he believes."

"What do you know about Ted?"

"Just what he told me. He grew up in St. Louis in The Hill neighborhood. His dad committed suicide when Ted was in his teens. His mother couldn't cope with raising him. Ted told me she had him committed to a state mental hospital. When he was eighteen, he was released back into her care. That was when he left and soon learned the ways of the homeless. He roams back and forth between St. Louis and Jackson, Mississippi."

"Do you think he might talk to me?" asked Jim.

"I don't know. He's pretty scared. He told me he was leaving for Mississippi. Says he has some family down there. He just wants to get out of here."

"Can you ask him for me?"

"He won't even see me anymore," Cotton said. "Says that everyone he knows is being followed. He won't take a chance."

"Thanks, Cotton. You're a good friend. I guess we better go get dinner ready. This crew looks pretty hungry. If you see Matt, will you point him out to me?"

"You can't miss him. Skinny white guy. Wears an Atlanta Braves ball cap."

In a little less than an hour, they had served twenty-six plates of meatloaf, with mashed potatoes and green beans. Matt never showed up.

"How many food bags do you make up these days?" Jim asked.

"I've been making twenty. They're usually gone before lunch."

"I'll stay and help you."

Once everyone left the dining area, Jim made the meatloaf sandwiches. Cotton added a bottle of water to each food bag, taped the bags shut, and stored them in the refrigerator. After helping Cotton clean up, Jim headed for home.

Night fell over Memphis—hot and humid, as was usual in June. From a third-floor window on Cotton Row, Ted watched moving specks of light cross the Mississippi River on the Hernando DeSoto Bridge. The streets appeared empty, but his fear of being found outweighed his need for nourishment. Lying down on a stack of corrugated paper boxes and newspapers, he closed his eyes and tried to sleep.

Looking over at the clock in his room, Cotton rolled out of bed. It was 2:24 AM. His sleep had been disturbed by the earlier conversation with Jim

Damos rotating through his mind. Sliding on his robe and slippers, Cotton retrieved a hidden pack of cigarettes and lighter from underneath his mattress. He unscrewed the emergency door fuse and exited the door from his room to the back alley.

The alley was black, except for a faint glow at one corner of the building from the adjacent street. Walking over to an overturned mop bucket, Cotton checked to see if Ted had claimed his food bag. Everything remained as he had left it hours ago. He picked up the bag and headed back into the darker part of the alley. Removing the water, Cotton pitched the bag into the open lid of a green Dumpster. Taking out his cigarettes, he struck his lighter. Shocked by a face staring at him with wild eyes, he dropped the cigarette from his mouth. In a split second, the flash of fire reflected off the Dumpster. Cotton stumbled backward and crumbled to the asphalt.

The call came in at 5:15 AM from the waste management driver. By eight thirty, the CSU team had combed the area and removed the body. Ballistics later confirmed that the barrel marking on the .38-caliber bullet was consistent with that of the Mangler's. The CSU team gathered no additional information.

"What do you think, Jack?" asked Dave, removing the security tapeline from across the alley's entrance.

"We've got a real situation with this Mangler," Jack replied. "We've got to find this person. Whoever it is, he or she is searching out homeless people. It leads me to believe that a homeless person has emotionally damaged this person or a member of this person's family."

"That would make sense," Dave said, "but I'm at a loss for a motive other than self-gratification."

"Well, if we're dealing with a deranged murderer who kills without any financial motive, then it has to be emotional. This Mangler is striking out at random, either for sexual stimulation or emotional revenge. Since there is no apparent sign of sexual abuse, it has to be for revenge."

"Okay, let's say it's for revenge. I don't know of anybody killed or robbed by a homeless person in the last year, do you, Jack?"

"Can't say I do, but it may not have happened here. All I know is that this Mangler is holding the homeless community responsible for something bad that happened."

Jack looked down the alley and saw Lou Cros walking toward them. "Lou, you're not supposed to be here. I've told you before, you need to stay out of this and let us do our job."

"I want to look through the alley," Lou said. "You either need to arrest me or get out of my way."

Jack took a deep breath and held his temper. "We've taken the tape down. We can't stop you from walking through the alley. Just stay out of our way. How did you find out about this, anyway?"

"I heard it on my police scanner this morning. I got over here as soon as I could. Do I have your permission to walk through the alley, Jack?"

Jack looked at the security tape in Dave's hand. "No law against walking through an alley. Just remember what I said."

"Thanks, Jack."

As the two officers began to leave, Jack addressed Lou once more. "If you find anything, call me. Will you do that?"

"Sure, Jack. You'll be the first to know."

Walking back to their patrol car, Dave broke the silence. "What's going on with Lou?"

"I don't know."

"Did you see how he was dressed? And his face looked like he hadn't slept for days."

"He looks pretty bad," agreed Jack. "I would guess he's back on the bottle. I hate to see him this way. He's had a hard go of things. It's time for him to call it quits. I think he was wrong to come back on duty when he did. I guess he felt he needed to do something or go crazy."

"I don't think it helped him," Dave said. "He looks pretty crazy right now."

Once Jack and Dave left the area, Lou paced the alleyway, looking at every small scrap of paper he could find. He noticed that the contents of the Dumpster had been removed, and blotches of fingerprint dusting freckled its side. Behind the Dumpster, along the mission wall, Lou spotted a red fragment of paper. Turning it over with his pen, it was easy to identify as a torn piece of Big Red chewing gum wrapper. The shock of reality weakened his knees. Leaning his back against the painted concrete block wall of the mission, he lowered his head and ran the murders through his mind. Mentally fighting with his conclusion, Lou found himself denying the evidence before him. Turning on his phone, he called Sue.

"Lou, where have you been? I've called a dozen times. Why won't you answer your phone?"

"I cut it off," replied Lou. "I didn't want to talk to anyone."

"Not even me?" Sue asked.

"Especially you."

There was a long silence on the phone before Sue spoke. "What do you mean by that? Is there something you need to tell me?"

"No, but there's something I need to ask you."

"I'm waiting."

"You know there was another murder before daylight this morning?"

"Yes, I heard. It is all over the airways, along with your suspension."

Taking a minute to get his courage up, Lou dropped the question. "I need to know where you were this morning."

"You jerk!" she burst out. "Do you actually think I had something to do with this? Who do you think you are? You're on suspension! I can't believe what I'm hearing!"

"I need to know. I just need to hear it from you."

"You won't hear it from me on the phone!" she screamed. "If you want to talk to me, you and your demented mind will have to face me!"

Lou wiped the sweat from his face. Closing his eyes, he applied finger pressure to the bridge of his nose. His head began to pound. A chill ran over his body. "Okay. Where can we meet?" he asked.

"I'll meet you in Cotton Row. In the alleyway you talked to me about, the one where you had your premonition."

"I can't do that! Don't make me do that!" he begged.

"If you're going to accuse me of something, you need to face me and your demons. I can stop all this. I can put your mind at rest. I can help you. Meet me there."

The phone went dead. Pushing Redial, Lou attempted to reach Sue again. She didn't answer. Walking back to his car on Riverside Drive, Lou sat in the front seat and stared out the windshield. The sun sparkled on the waves breaking against the muddy shoreline at the river's edge. Lou recalled riding the Mississippi River aboard the *Memphis Queen* for a police award dinner cruise.

Sue was there that night. She was dressed in a pale violet dress. Her hair was short then, with small curls that turned in toward her cheeks. She was happy that night, laughing and joking with all her fellow officers. She sat next to him during dinner. Several times she laughed and touched his arm. After dinner, they went outside along the deck. The lights of the city illuminated the dark surface of the muddy water. He leaned against her shoulder and spoke over the sound of the music. He would never forget the fresh smell of her body.

Today, his world had changed. Glancing into the rearview mirror, he could hardly recognize himself. He had the stubble of an unshaven beard, his hair was oily and unkempt, and his face was bruised. He looked into his own eyes in the mirror, noting that they were vacant and bloodshot, crisscrossed with small red veins running through the whites around his dark pupils. Lou wiped a tear from his cheek and made his decision. With shaking hands, he left his car and opened the trunk. He removed a gun that was taped inside his spare tire well and headed toward Cotton Row.

Hidden in a clump of trees a short distance away, Rocky stood still, fully enveloped in shadows. He watched Lou, and he smiled, pleased with what he saw.

CHAPTER 15

Sue

LOU TURNED THE CORNER into the familiar alleyway of Cotton Row. Taken by surprise, he spotted Matt standing below a rusted drop-down fire escape ladder in the middle of the building. Matt was looking up at the second-floor window and talking on his cell phone. Lou approached just as he closed the phone.

"Get lost, Cros. You're not wanted here," Matt said, holding up his arm to block Lou's advance.

"You back off!" Lou said. "I have every right to be here."

"No, you don't. You're on suspension," Matt said, and he pushed Lou backward. "This is official police business. You're not welcome."

"What kind of business?" inquired Lou, taking the shove without a response. He didn't want to get in Matt's face, although he was becoming angry. He hoped to get more information.

"I saw someone in the second floor window," Matt said. "I think it's Ted. I just called for backup. They'll be here any minute. You need to step down and leave the area, or I'll arrest you for interference," warned Matt.

All Lou could think about was that it might be Sue inside the building. He needed to get inside first. Pointing toward the end of the building, Lou lied to Matt in order to catch him off balance. "There's your backup now."

Just as Matt turned around to look, Lou pulled his gun from his pants pocket and struck Matt on the back of the head, knocking him unconscious.

Lou saw an old broom in a pile of trash, grabbed it, and used it to reach the hinged section of stairs at the bottom of the fire escape. He pulled the stairs down and climbed to the second-floor emergency door. He pushed the door open and slowly entered the building.

Within minutes, Jack and Dave pulled to the curb in front of the alleyway entrance. Once they left their patrol car, they rushed to the body lying in the alley. As Matt revived, he recognized the two officers. "Cros hit me in the head. I think he went into the building. I think Ted is in there."

"You want me to call an ambulance?" asked Jack.

"No, I'll be okay, but I feel pretty dizzy," Matt said, leaning his back against the building. "You guys need to go ahead inside. I'll wait here."

Another figure entered the alley. Jack crouched down and pulled his gun. "Police!" he shouted. "Hands in the air and identify yourself!"

Rocky stopped his entry and lifted his hand into the air. "I'm Special Agent Jon Chevros! FBI! We have been given jurisdiction with the Mangler case. Your Captain Smitters should have contacted you."

Jack holstered his gun and stood up. "Yes, I did receive that information a short time ago. Captain Smitters asked us to assist."

The agent advanced into the alley. "I want backup to cover the perimeter of this building," he said, immediately taking charge of the situation, which Jack didn't like. But there was nothing he could do about it. "Once the perimeter is secure," Chevros continued, "I want both of you to enter through the front door and check the first floor. I'll enter from the fire escape on the second floor and meet you at the second-floor stairwell when I'm through. We'll then split up and take the third floor from both sides of the building." Looking over at Matt, Chevros said, "I believe you're Jim Lovell. Are you okay to cover the fire escape?"

"Yes, I'll be fine."

"Do you know if Lou is armed?" Chevros asked.

"I didn't see a gun. But he hit me with something," Jim replied.

"Then we have to assume he is," Chevros said. "Anyone have any questions?"

"No questions," Jack said. "We're good to go."

"Let's roll! I'm going in now. As soon as your backup has the building covered, hit the front."

Everyone nodded in agreement, and the plan was set in motion. In four minutes, two more patrol cars arrived at the scene. Jack gave the officers their instructions and then proceeded to the front door. Using his billy club, he was able to pry the hasp off the rotted wooden door. Pulling their guns, Jack and Dave carefully entered the first floor. The building smelled musty. The air was sour and still. The wooden floor was cluttered with old papers and trash. Large chips of white paint hung from the plaster ceiling. Just enough light was penetrating the darkened windows to allow adequate vision. An old reception desk was situated in the center of the floor. A pair of bronze elevator doors stood out against the dirty whitewashed back wall. Two large warped glass directories hung twisted on either side of the plate. Restrooms were located on both sides of the elevator doors. A matching pair of wooden stairs completed the back corners.

Jack and Dave took positions on either side of the first office door. Jack pushed open the door with his foot and waited for any sound that might declare someone's presence. Hearing no movement, Jack slipped into the office while Dave remained on guard. With the help of his flashlight, Jack moved quickly through the dimly lit entry and adjoining rooms. The office was empty. Alternating their positions, Dave searched the next office. Once they were satisfied that the six offices were clear, they searched the restrooms and janitor's closet. The first floor was empty. Next, the two officers separated, and each took a set of stairs. As Jack turned the corner at the first landing, a dark shadow arched its back and announced its presence with a sinister hiss. Jack fanned his flashlight and pistol toward the sound. The beams of light from the flashlight were reflected in Mr. Nobody's eyes. Jack jumped against the stairwell wall as the cat brushed past his leg. Leaning his body against the plaster, he gave a sigh of relief as his racing pulse began to slow down. Reaching the second floor, he was met by Dave and Jon Chevros.

"Anything to report?" Jack asked.

"Nothing," Dave said.

"Second floor is clear," Chevros stated. "Any questions?"

"No, sir," Dave said.

Chevros nodded as a message to proceed and moved to the set of stairs at the far end of the floor.

Together again as a pair, Jack and Dave advanced to the top floor. The third floor was used as a warehouse. The floor was filled with old cotton grading tables stacked on top of each other, along with stored sales desks, chairs, filing cabinets, old Coke machines, and refrigerators. The room had a musty odor, like that of a dusty street after a rain. Hanging light fixtures dangled from the exposed ceiling. The height and maze of the supplies completely blocked out the light in most areas and made it very difficult to move around.

Once the three men were in place at the back wall, Chevros shouted, "FBI. Come out with your hands above your head! *Now!*"

Close to the front of the room, a chair was bumped off the top of a table and hit the floor with a bang. Shuffling was heard across the wooden floor, and then silence.

"Lou, it's Jack Mills. We're here to help. You need to step out where we can see you."

"Get out, Jack!" Lou cried. "Get out while you can!"

Jon Chevros motioned to Jack with his hand to continue talking so he could get a feel for Lou's location.

"Lou, we're here to help you. What's going on?"

"The Mangler. She's here. She's after Ted."

Jon nodded at Jack and started creeping between the furniture toward the sound.

"Who, Lou? Who is here?"

"The Mangler. It's Sue. I know it's her. She is out to kill Ted."

Dave glanced at Jack with a stunned look on his face. "Did he say, *Sue?* Does he mean *Sue Nash?*"

"Nobody's going to be killed, Lou. We've already called for backup," said Jack. "You need to show yourself so we can help."

"Go away, Jack. I have to do this. I have to settle this."

Jack watched as Jon worked his way along the sidewall. Jack could see a body curled up in the front corner under a desk. He was able to identify it as Ted. Lou's voice was coming from the other side, below one of the windows. As Chevros got closer to Ted's body, he crouched down and raised his index finger in front of his lips to ask for silence. Ted pulled his knees to his chest to form a small ball.

"Lou, you said Sue is here. Do you mean Sue Nash?" asked Jack.

"She's the Mangler, Jack. She's here to kill Ted. I have her trapped. She can't get out. Leave us alone. I have to end the killing. Stay away, Jack. I have to do this," Lou yelled.

Dave looked at Jack again. "He said Sue Nash. He believes she's here."

"The man is really sick, Dave. I was called to the crime scene the day she was killed. It's been almost a year."

Jack and Dave started to advance along the outside wall.

"Lou, it's Jack. Sue isn't here. I was with you the day she was killed. She's gone, Lou. Come on out. Everything is okay. We can help."

"She is here!" Lou screamed. "I can see her."

Lou wiped his clammy hands on his dirty pants and tightened his grip on the .38. Beads of sweat ran down the sides of his face and disappeared into his damp collar. Pressing his back against the wall, he had a clear view of Sue. She was dressed in blue jeans and a light blue shirt. Her hair was pulled back and tied in with a white sash. Sue smiled as she approached him.

"I know what you've done," Lou said. "I know you're the Mangler. I can't let you kill anymore. It has to end here." Placing both shaking hands on the gun, he raised it to eye level. Dark figures started to appear from behind the clutter of furniture. Torn rags covered their skeletal bodies. White strands of hair hung down their faces. Their eye sockets were empty and black. For a split second, Sue's face morphed to one of equal horror, but then it returned to the way she had always looked.

"You were always smart," Sue said. "You were the very best. But this isn't about me, Lou. It's about you."

"Tell them to get back!" Lou motioned toward the advancing apparitions. "They can't have you! I won't let them have you!"

"They're not here for me. They're here to settle your account. They want to give you rest. You do want to stop your pain, don't you, Lou? I can help. I can end your torture."

"I just want it to be like it used to be. I want the pain to stop. I want us to be together like before." Lou grabbed his head. His face wrenched in pain.

"Who the hell is he talking to?" Dave asked.

"He's talking to himself," Jack said.

Jack watched as Chevros got down and slowly crawled across the dusty floor. Lou was pressed behind an upright office desk. Jack estimated that Chevros was twenty-five feet away from Lou when he identified himself. "Special Agent Jon Chevros! FBI! Come out and put your hands on your head!"

Sue looked at Lou and continued to talk. "The police are here for you. They'll put you away. You don't want that to happen, do you?"

"Stop it!" Lou insisted, turning the gun on her. "You're the one they're after! You killed those people! You're trying to confuse me! I'm here to stop you!"

"You're wrong, Lou. You know I could never do that. You know the truth."

Lou grabbed his head again as the pain intensified. "I can stop you. I can stop your killing."

Sue took Lou by his gun hand and placed it next to his temple. "Do you want to be with me?" she asked.

"Yes, I want to be with you always."

The blast echoed off the exposed ceiling. Ted screamed from the sound and began to weep.

EPILOGUE

CAPTAIN SMITTERS LOOKED AT the people seated around the conference room table. To his left was Special Agent Jon Chevros. Next to him was Jim Lovell, the police undercover agent known as Matt. To the captain's right were Officers Jack Mills and Dave Drake. Looking through a four-inch-thick file folder, Smitters took a sip of coffee, made a face, and pushed the cup aside. "I think you all know each other by now," he said.

The group nodded.

"I want to thank Special Agent Chevros for his assistance in this case, and I would like him to bring us up to date with current information."

"Thanks, Captain." Agent Chevros paused briefly, and flipped through some papers that were in front of him. "The FBI was called in to assist the ATF in this case. The original involvement was centered on James Henry, a.k.a. Glitter, and his family pawnshop operation. We had information that illegal weapons were being sold and transported across state lines. There was also evidence that stolen jewelry was being melted down and used to back up a money laundering scam.

"John's Pawnshop was the front for this operation. John Henry, James's older brother, ran the shop and was directly involved in the gun-trafficking and money laundering operation. The younger brother, Philip, a.k.a. Little G, was recently employed as their bookkeeper, but at this time, we haven't determined if he was involved in the money laundering. Indictments were issued on all three brothers. James and John Henry are being held without bail at the Criminal Justice Center. Philip Henry has been released on bond and will most likely be put on probation.

"The crossover investigation came about with the relationship between Detective Lou Cros and James Henry. An investigation was opened on Detective Lou Cros with the full cooperation of the mayor and the Memphis Police Department, with Captain Smitters on point.

"After Detective Cros's suicide, a search of his house revealed evidence that linked him to the murders of the homeless men in the city. Ballistics run on the .38-caliber Smith & Wesson model 10 handgun we found in his home matched the ones for the gun used on the victims. Some blood splatters were removed from the gun, which will be matched for DNA." Agent Chevros paused, checked his notes, and continued.

"Several prescriptions of Seroquel, an antipsychotic medication, along with lithium, Depakote, and Valium were also present in his house. The prescriptions were dated shortly after Officer Sue Nash's death. Most of the bottles were unused. We have subpoenaed his medical records, and we are awaiting their delivery. We also found several family pictures of him as a small boy. His father's head was either cut out or scratched off the photo.

"We found a shrine to Officer Sue Nash in Detective Cros's bedroom. As you well know, she was killed in the line of duty a little over a year ago, and it looks as though Detective Cros blamed himself for her death or at least was so in love with her he couldn't get over it. Newspaper articles, pictures, and keepsakes from the last five years are pinned and taped to the wall. I'm hoping someone here can fill me in on Officer Nash." The agent leaned back in his chair and turned the conference back over to Captain Smitters.

The captain pulled another case file over in front of him and opened it to a set tab. "Jack, you were at the scene of Officer Nash's death. Will you enlighten Special Agent Chevros about that day?"

Jack recalled the incident. "Dave was off that week, and I was listed for backup duty. I received a call from dispatch asking for officer assistance at the old GE manufacturing facility on Riverside Drive. When I arrived, Lou Cros and Sue Nash were waiting outside. Lou informed me that a drug deal was going down, and he asked me to assist by covering the inside exits. We entered the building from the side and made our way to a back wall office, where we could hear conversation. The three of us spread out."

"Would you explain where each of you were located in relation to the office?" Captain Smitters asked.

"Sue took cover behind a concrete pillar on the north side of the office. I was stationed on the south side, and Lou was in the middle and closest to the office door. A heavily tattooed man lingered outside. From my vantage point, I could see that he had a revolver stuck inside his belt. Lou shouted out our presence and ordered the man to raise his hands and drop to his knees. Just as the man followed Lou's instructions, the lights inside the office went out. A metal chair burst through an office window, and a couple of rounds were fired from inside."

Jack looked down at the table. Captain Smitters could tell that recalling the incident was emotional for him.

"Please continue."

"The office door slammed open, and two men exited, firing rounds in Lou's direction. Officer Nash and I returned fire, wounding one of the men. Once the other one realized he was in a cross fire he dropped his gun and surrendered. When Officer Nash stepped out from behind the pillar, a homeless man frightened by the gunfire ran right into the middle of the mess. Seeing that Officer Nash was distracted, the man that was kneeling down pulled his gun and fired two shots. As Officer Nash pushed the homeless man out of the way, she took a hit above her vest into the throat area. Lou immediately returned fire and took the shooter out.

"Lou was devastated by Officer Nash's death. He had a mental breakdown, and he was on a leave of absence for eight months. I was surprised when he came back to work. The loss consumed him. In his day, Lou was one of the best detectives on the force. My guess is that in his recent mental state, he held the homeless community responsible for her death."

"You sound like you're defending him," Jim Lovell commented, his voice thick with anger.

Jack felt his face turn red. His voice became elevated. "Lou was a friend. His mind snapped after his breakdown. I hold myself partly responsible for not seeing some of the warning signs. And just for the record, Mr. Lovell, it would take ten of you to even get close to being the detective that Lou was!"

"That's enough, Jack," Captain Smitters said. "I'm sure Officer Lovell meant no disrespect. Isn't that right, Officer Lovell?"

Jim Lovell looked away from Jack. Slouching in his chair and appearing small, Lovell said, "Yes, Captain, that's right."

"Good. Any other questions?" asked Captain Smitters.

Officer Dave Drake cleared his throat. "What can you tell us about Ted?"

"Ted is currently at the Tennessee Psychiatric Hospital," answered Captain Smitters. "Our interview with him went poorly. Ted suffers from epilepsy and schizophrenia. He has been without medication for quite some time. In his current state of mind, we were unable to gain any real information. We did find out that he was at the scene of the Firestone plant murder. We have to assume that he might have seen Lou Cros that night. This would explain Lou's obsession with finding him. We were able to locate some of Ted Meyer's family in Jackson, Mississippi, who have agreed to pick him up. His attending psychiatrist has hopes that with family care and medication, he will be okay. Jim, you were at the mission. What information do you have about the man called Cotton?"

Jim Lovell leaned forward in his chair. "Cotton had befriended Ted while he was at the mission. I believe that Lou was hanging out there looking for Ted the night Cotton was murdered. I think Cotton was just in the wrong place at the wrong time."

"Thanks, Jim," Captain Smitters said. "That brings us to Gary West, a.k.a. Bones. Without ballistics, we're unable to tie his death to the others. His murder will continue to be listed as a drug-related incident unless new information is obtained. We can connect him to the Henry brothers and his clash with Lou Cros. Most likely, West probably provoked Cros to the point where Cros killed him.

"A bit of good news is that Jim Demos has taken a part-time job back at the Union Avenue Mission. He will be working with Mr. Johnson, and he will be starting a new citywide outreach program for the homeless that has been very successful in New Orleans. The mayor's office has made a commitment to get involved in fund-raising for the expansion of the mission, along with assistance from the local churches to address the homeless issue." Captain Smitters closed his folder and looked around the room. "Anything else?" Since there were no more questions, the captain stood up. "Thanks again to everyone. Now, let's get back to work."

Jack and Dave left the precinct and got into their patrol car. Neither of them spoke as they drove down Union Avenue. Approaching the Union Avenue Mission, Jack pulled over to the curb. Putting both hands on top of the steering wheel, he stared out the side window. His emotions were disjointed. He felt distressed and relieved at the same time.

"I should have done something."

"Jack, there was no way you could have known what was going on in his mind. Lou was sick. You had no control of that."

Jack nodded in agreement and forced a smile. "Yeah, you're right. Thanks."

Jack put the patrol car in gear and continued down Union Avenue. Pulling into the Beale Street District, Jack crossed over Front Street and parked on Riverside Drive. The two officers walked in silence, inching along the cracked sidewalk. As they approached Cotton Row, Jack stopped and stared at the empty buildings. His body felt drained. It was hard for him to accept the fact that he couldn't have done anything, but he knew it was true. Lou was haunted by demons of his past. The ghosts that wander through our minds and steal into our dreams had consumed Lou's tormented mind.

Jack looked at the third floor of the building he knew too well. His memories of that night would always be with him. He could not escape his past. He knew that Lou Cros, Sue Nash, and the homeless people who died at Lou's hand were now among the merchants and porters that once walked the offices and streets and made their living in part from the majestic and muddy Mississippi River and all it brought to Memphis—the people that now walked in Jack's mind and would forever be remembered as the ghosts of Cotton Row.